BIPOLAR NATION

Will the REAL Majority Please Stand Up?

AUSTIN L. PEARL

Lido Publishing ΔΔΔ Washington DC & New York

Published in the United States by Lido Publishing, a Limited Liability Corporation with offices in Washington and New York. For more information please contact Lido Publishing:
Phone: (202) 486-5282
Phone: (516) 369-6733
E-mail: lidopublications@gmail.com

Interior illustrations created by Austin Pearl and sketched by Mr. Stephen Nagy, Freelance Illustrator for hire (contact: nagystudios@yahoo.com). Cover also created by Austin Pearl, but graciously revised and retouched by Mr. Jason Tuchman of Pistol Studios (contact: jason@pistolstudios.com). P25695-23: Official Portrait of President George W. Bush courtesy of George W. Bush Presidential Library. Definitions from The Free Dictionary reprinted with permission from Farlex, Inc. Definitions from Skepticwiki.org reprinted with permission from proprietor of Skepticwiki.org.

Edited by P.R.
Library of Congress Control Number: 2010912697
ISBN-13: 978-0-615-39774-0
ISBN-10: 0615397743

For my mother, Bonnie Miller, who endured every hardship so that I would have everything… and for my father, Irwin Pearl, who raised me to believe that the possibilities are truly boundless.

Contents

Introduction

Over the past several years I've noticed what can only be described as a phenomenon. It always existed but in the years after 9/11 it seemed to grow and solidify manifold. Although it first became apparent to many via the vitriolic back and forth over health care reform during the summer of 2009, that experience was merely a symptom vice a cause. I like to think that because I live in a major city where different people and ideas come together, or in this case scream at one another, I simply saw it coming before most.

People in America now HATE each other. It's not black versus white or North versus South. It's 'liberals' versus 'conservatives', Republicans versus Democrats, and 'progressives' versus 'the right'. Imaginary lines have been drawn, walls have been built (primarily around brains), and intellectual war has been declared. While America used to be a nation of bi-partisanship, today it is bipolar. Whereas the former denotes having different viewpoints but ultimately working together, the latter denotes a deeply troubling psychological issue.

Consider this: The bases of the two largest political parties in America today believe that the other represents the biggest danger to that very same country. They each just happen to disagree on every single major issue! Keep that in mind, those words if you will: *"...every single major issue".* It is my hope that if you are reading this you are one of them, because the point of this book is to talk you down. The point of this book is to illuminate for you the sheer improbability that two individuals, let alone millions, disagree on everything! But most importantly, the point is to show the damage you are doing by choosing a side and touting the party line. This book will be like a mirror: YOU should be on the cover.

I am concerned for the future of our county and feel compelled to speak out. Since those dark days after 9/11 our nation's political fortunes have taken severe twists and turns. The net result has been akin to a giant political centrifuge: All that's left are the lunatics! BIPOLAR NATION seeks to get beyond the superficial and sensationalized political arguments flying around the airwaves and answer the pivotal questions of our times: How did things get this bad? How did America turn into a country that hates itself? But perhaps most importantly, what will our future hold if we continue to fracture along political lines? How is this impacting America's future, its place in the world?

The answers to these questions lay not only with those who profit from a terrified, angry, and divided America; but within ourselves as a people. The individual psychological and by extension collective intellectual deadlock in which we find ourselves is truly the struggle of our times. We need to take a breath and re-trace our steps before re-entering that voting booth…

I ask that you read this book with an open mind (I apologize for employing the most overused, rhetorical, and might I say misunderstood phrase in the universe. If you normally define yourself as such, then I really implore you to read on), because we are going on a journey together. This journey will answer questions about ourselves as a people, the psychology behind political polarization, the true nature of bias in our media, and the very future of our great country.

We will begin by asking you some simple questions about your own political ideology. These questions are intended to set the stage for a jolt to your inner biases and thought patterns vis-à-vis all things political—regardless of your persuasion. The intent is not to prove you wrong, but merely to open that door that is your mind… if only by a crack.

Then, we will re-trace America's steps by exploring the psychology behind extreme partisanship, tracing its roots to a nexus of natural human tendencies and the two party system itself. What you think is not nearly as important as how you think. Because if you are not aware of how you think, you simply cannot trust that which you do.

Once we understand how we think, we will explore the grim reality that is the new American media. Is it liberal? Is it conservative? Ha… Such accusations have become insulting to the intelligence! A well *honed partisan industry* that caters to **both sides** now effectively filters and sets the standards for America's political discourse. We must identify, define, and label this industry in an ideologically blind manner… because to accuse one side of bias without recognizing the misdeeds of the other is to implicitly take sides. To do so at this point is to be culpable in America's decline.

And thus, we will then—as a people—declare intellectual war upon the new media establishment. This can only be accomplished by exposing the true methodologies of the politically biased, once and for all sweeping aside that pathetic and simplistic notion that they rely on little things called 'lies' to present the news with an ideological bent. But perhaps more importantly, we will recognize the depth of political bias in our media emanating from both sides of the spectrum. So put your biases aside and be ready for truth vice more partisan rhetoric; this is WAR for the soul of our country and its future!

Our introspection of how America reached this intellectual quagmire will lead us to an exercise: The bases of both parties truly believe that if and only if they had uninhibited control of America's governance, our society would be perfect. But what would such a state of affairs actually look like? How did America reach such a level of political moderation in the first place (relevant to other nations—certainly you have the common sense to look elsewhere to better understand yourself, RIGHT)? We as a nation need to take a hard look at the reality that would exist should either party achieve its dream. But we also need to think long and hard about why it is that the partisan dream of absolute power will NEVER happen…

This entire work—this exercise of the brain—culminates in an outlook, a prediction if you will: What might the future hold if America continues to fracture along political lines? What are the worst and best case scenarios? Is it actually possible that political instability—a term usually reserved to describe the state of affairs in third world countries—can occur inside the United States of America? Regardless and in the spirit of John F. Kennedy, I'll tell you what YOU can do for your country to avoid anything broaching that outcome. Extreme partisanship can be defeated, but it will require a somewhat unique political upheaval. *It starts inside your head...*

-Austin

P.S. It's time I told you that if you want to read something that simply reaffirms your political views, grab one of the other countless books sitting on store shelves today. They are just overflowing with partisan drivel that caters precisely to your needs for re-enforcement. If I do take some of your time, it will be for the sake of reason and truth.

DISCLAIMER(S)

OFFICIAL: All views and opinions expressed herein are the author's alone, and do not reflect any positions, official or otherwise of the United States Department of Defense (case number 10-331).

POLITICAL: Please do not use any of the examples provided in this book for political purposes. Taken out of context or as cherry picked passages, one can easily make this book sound partisan in nature. That is precisely the opposite of the intent. The examples provided are solely utilized to educate and inform the reader about the role of extreme partisanship and its perpetuators in our society—not bolster a political position or provide either 'side' with ammunition. And henceforth, you will not find an example of one political party or pundit employing political tactics or rhetoric without one from the other.

Speak truth to power...
—A Retired Army Colonel

In this case you, the American people, are that power...

CHAPTER 1: Getting To Know You

Your political views are intellectually and morally inconsistent, meaning they have no intellectual cohesion, and I can prove it if you are willing to listen...

Before we get to it, I want to be clear: Being a partisan hack should be considered akin to having a psychological issue. It is something that as we will later explore, builds up and is re-enforced over the course of years and therefore is extraordinarily difficult to undo. Signs you are nothing but a partisan hack (as opposed to an informed individual or great thinker) include the following:

- You have a prepackaged and negative judgment of any and all actions of members of the opposing political party
- You easily become emotional or agitated when engaged in political discussions or debates
- You regularly watch, listen to, or read material from a partisan pundit, network, or website. I will not name any (yet), but these individuals and organizations are easily identifiable once you are attuned to their characteristics. They are distinguishable by their comprehensive defense of their political party of choice, regardless of how indefensible the action or policy in question
- You often denounce those who oppose your positions as 'communists' or 'fascists' (currently being substituted with 'socialist' and 'racist')

- Perhaps most importantly, you find yourself uncomfortably reaching to defend the actions and policies of your political party or individuals within it

In order to raise awareness of the aforementioned condition and hopefully begin to roll back its effects, we're going to document it for the first time. I hereby declare the existence of... the partisan sickness. It is defined as: a condition in which the patient has a prepackaged negative judgment of any and all actions of the members of the opposing political party; often resulting in unpleasant dinner party conversations, emotional arguments, and a higher than normal usage rate of the terms 'fascist' or 'communist' (currently being substituted with 'socialist' and 'racist').

The first step towards rehabilitation, as always, is to admit you have a problem. So, let's start with an introspective look at you, the reader. How do you reach political conclusions? Do you have a political philosophy that guides your political decisions? Surely you don't believe that your political decisions (you know, those most important decisions that impact the lives of everyone else) are random in nature, right? If they were random that would mean you reach them not unlike a child choosing between two completely identical pieces of candy.

But what if I could prove to you that there is no common glue between your political views? What if I could prove that much of your political views—despite holding them as deeply held beliefs—are arbitrary? (Arbitrary meaning "illogical" and "random").

Let's take a test. I need not only your undivided attention, but more importantly an open mind (you DO consider yourself "open minded", right?) If you're a Democrat or Progressive, please go to question set "A". If you're a Republican or Conservative, please skip down to question set "B". Please don't read the other question set. Not yet at least. This isn't about 'them'; it is about you.

A

(1) Do you believe that government should ensure citizens have access to health care?
(2) Do you believe the government should seek to correct economic inequality among its citizens?
(3) Do you believe government should assertively regulate 'corporate agreed'?

(4) Do you believe the government should have the ability to wiretap, without a warrant, the phones of individuals believed to be engaging in terrorist activity?

If your answers were (1) Yes, (2) Yes, (3) Yes, and (4) Yes; there may be some hope for you, as at least you can stand on your own two legs (albeit shaky ones since you obviously have no faith in mankind). But unfortunately in today's America—if you went to question set A, your answers were more likely as follows: (1) Yes, (2) Yes, (3) Yes, (4) No.

Let me explain: You believe that government should play a large role in society, ensuring health coverage and closely regulating the market to ensure the citizens do not suffer inequality. The government is the ultimate arbiter because it is not for profit and elected by the people. Yet it should not retain the ability to monitor those who may be conspiring (perhaps imminently) to crash planes into buildings? You may be rationalizing your answer right now—but I implore you to read on. Here's another one:

(1) Do you think people should be able to do as they please sexually?
(2) Do you believe that a woman should have the right to choose whether or not to have an abortion?
(3) Do you believe in freedom of speech?
(4) Do you believe that the more money one makes the more they should be taxed?

So let me get this straight: Socially, people should be allowed to do anything they want. After all, one's right to decide their sexuality is a civil right. The right to an abortion is in part a safeguard against gender discrimination, but also a freedom of the individual—the freedom to choose what to do with one's own body.

However, it is not within someone's right to start a business and be successful without the government successively taking more of their money? What is the difference between one's "social" choices and choices vis-à-vis work? (Note that I could not think of a category akin to "social" in which to place the gamut of educational and professional choices one makes that in turn lead to making more money). Are that individual's civil rights not being violated? What about individual financial freedom? How come financial freedom doesn't go with reproduction, marriage, and speech? Why is one private and the other everyone else's business?

Right now you are probably rationalizing that the individual who makes more money owes a debt to society, or perhaps attained their money through inherently unfair circumstances. The very fact that you have to rationalize should indicate that your positions are not infallible. But more importantly (as I am not seeking to argue whether your actual positions are wrong or right), I want to know: How did you arrive at these conclusions? Are you an intelligent thinker as you so often posit, or are your political positions random in nature?

I mean, you argue the government has this enormous role to play in society, except when people are seeking to crash planes into buildings. You then argue that individual freedom only exists in the realm of social issues. These are random or cherry picked positions (for which one has to rationalize quite strongly). How did these strongly entrenched positions end up in the same intellectual basket—or same category—"liberal" positions?

Random would imply that most other people who took the same test came up with a completely different set of answers (A few yes's, a few no's, etc). Yet somehow or another, the overwhelming majority of people who chose question set 'A' came up with the same (philosophically random—if not contradictory) answers. So the real point of the test, being that while your answers are technically random since they are not part of any consistent political philosophy or ideology (much like you wouldn't group an apple with vegetables or a salad crouton with giant fictionalized Japanese monsters), is that somehow everyone else got the same answers as you!

I will repeat this throughout the book: I am not supporting or opposing any of your actual positions but merely asking you to ponder how you reach them in the first place. The truth (which you may be rationalizing to avoid) is that your answers are intellectually (and morally if you want to go there, although I am an agnostic New Yorker who has no morals) inconsistent. Therefore we must ask ourselves a logical question: Is it possible, just possible—that if you provided the same philosophically random if not contradictory answers as everyone else—that you are not thinking for yourself?

Before you get mad, relax! This book is not about blame, and as you will see it most definitely not about hate. This book seeks to get beyond the negativity that has so pervaded American political discourse and examine what is driving huge numbers of Americans to engage in vicious dinner time discussions with their family members and vote primarily to get the other guy out of office (as opposed to endorsing the new guy's policies). But to do so, we all must first reflect on ourselves. In fact as I'm sure you will now inevitably read the "B" question subset—you know, for the guy who just happens to think the complete opposite of everything you do—you will see that this book is an equal opportunity mechanism. Nobody will be spared, everybody will be given a chance, and hopefully we'll all be better off because of it. In fact, read her/his section and I'll meet up with you at the end. Oh, and while you're there, answer his/her questions will ya'?

B

(1) Do you believe that private property rights should be absolute?
(2) Do you believe that people should make their own decisions—as long as they're not harming others?
(3) Do you believe that government interference in the lives of the individual should only occur when absolutely necessary?
(4) Do you think Marijuana should be legal?

If your answers were (1) Yes, (2) Yes, (3) Yes, and (4) Yes, there may be some hope for you in that at least you are consistent. In fact, there may be no need for you to read this book (although speaking in terms of probability, I doubt it). Not because I am endorsing your positions but because you may have a consistent set of intellectual principles with which you generally adhere when making political decisions. Unfortunately your answers were more likely as follows: (1) Yes, (2) Yes, (3) Yes, and (4) No. And there are many 'social issues' (i.e. matters pertaining to the individual's private life) with which I could have substituted for marijuana.

But in case you still don't get it, let me spell it out for you: You believe that private property is exactly that—private. You believe that the individual is the ultimate actor in society and that the government should generally speaking, mind its own business. Yet others should not be allowed to smoke marijuana in their own homes? No one is saying that your kid's school bus driver should be allowed to smoke a joint before doing his morning rounds. But what I am saying, and on this I thought we agreed, are that others should be free to choose! Let me pre-empt your ongoing rationalization of your answer set: Alcohol arguably has a much worse effect on society. Your kid already has tried pot. Legalizing it would bolster the position that health is largely a matter of choice. The government should not control people's lives. How about we administer another test, to see if you got past the first one yet actually are a political hack... or even worse as all those leftists say you are—a racist!

(1) Was President Obama right to initiate the closure of the Guantanamo Bay detention center?
(2) Did President Obama's stimulus plan help the economy?
(3) Was President Obama right to announce a withdrawal date of U.S. forces from Iraq?
(4) Was President Obama right to re-initiate financial aid to organizations which promote birth control?

Well, I might as well ask you: Has President Obama ever done anything right in his entire life? And if not, what is the sheer probability that you disagree with every single decision one person has ever made? Now, what is important to note is that this last question set has no ideological cohesion. In other words, a certain set of answers would not place the reader on the side of one political philosophy or the other (i.e. less government versus more government). Just like the actions to which they pertain, the questions are random. So unlike the previous question set, there is no 'catch' question; 'catch' meaning that a certain answer would intellectually and morally contradict all of those previously given.

Yet you just happened to disagree with all of the President's positions anyway. So let's think this through. There is no method to the questioning here. The only thing the questions have in common is that they all concern positions taken up by our President; yet you somehow disagreed with all of them. My conclusion? Either you have a pre-conceived notion about every decision the man makes, or you actually are a racist like those liberals say you are! Hahaha! Please forgive me, it's just that I find it incredibly convenient how easily liberals throw around accusations of racism. Sometimes I wonder: Are they just trying to paint opponents of certain policies as racist? Or are their views just so pathologically ingrained that they honestly believe there can be no other explanation for the existence of an opposition?

But then again, here we have a case where someone does inexplicably disagree with everything President Obama does… hmmm. Maybe they're right? Nah, I'll give you the benefit of the doubt. At best you have the partisan sickness, at worst you are a racist. But just to make sure you understand that this book is an equal opportunity mechanism and that I'm not part of the 'liberal' or 'elite media', go back and read question set 'A'. This is what being fair and balanced actually looks like!

Come together…

Liberal: You're not going to believe this, but your cousin (I'm going to start calling the other guy "your cousin" from this point on) does not agree with one single policy of the President's. Don't you find it ridiculous that he automatically opposes everything President Obama does? Oh, but wait a minute, what were your answers? You agreed with every one of his decisions… What is the probability that President Obama has done every single thing right? Wow, liberals and conservatives never agree! Even when the issues at hand cannot be categorized…

Do you both get my point yet? So let me ask you: What is the probability that two people disagree on EVERY SINGLE MAJOR ISSUE? Forget the actual issues and just think about this from the point of view of probability and you will realize that it is actually IMPROBABLE that any two people disagree on everything. Yet your very brand of political thought, which I believe we deduced as random since there is no actual consistent political philosophy guiding it, has swept a huge segment of the population. It's sort of an intellectual enslavement to the party line.

And when I say "brand" I do mean brand, not unlike Coke or Pepsi. These days the two main political ideologies are being neatly bottled, packaged, and sold. The Engineers who design and perpetuate these 'ideas' are a few thinkers on the Left and Right, the factories that produce them are the Democratic and Republican National Parties, and the distributors the New York Times, Rush Limbaugh, MSNBC, Fox News, and the blogoshpere.

Now that we've completed our exercise (and I hope you are still here, I know how sensitive and self righteous partisan hacks can be), where do we go next? I have an idea. Allow me to introduce some concepts from another discipline, outside of the… um… political commentary discipline (PCD…yep) altogether. If you're not convinced yet that you have no real methodology in arriving at political decisions other than to support the party line after Chapter 2, you can exchange this book for some partisan drivel.

CHAPTER 2: American Political Psychology

Now I'll show you how we became intellectually and morally inconsistent. Extreme partisanship is inherent in the two party system and very quickly takes on psychological dimensions. It pressures you to take on and defend views that were not your own.

The real point of the exercises we did in Chapter 1 was to force that door open that is your mind, even if just by a crack. It wasn't to convince you to abandon all of your beliefs or change them. It was merely to nudge you outside of your default thought pattern. By questioning your own beliefs you are being truly open minded. Many have bought into the notion that you are open-minded if you subscribe to one set of political views as opposed to another. That is patently absurd and nothing but a simple way to reassure one's self of the validity of their views. I pose questions like the ones in Chapter 1 all the time, especially when I get into a discussion or debate with someone who consistently argues on behalf of the same political party regardless of the issue.

If I am asking questions of a certain ideological bend, such as big government versus small government, the subject almost always gives answers that are philosophically and intellectually inconsistent. If I ask questions about the actions or positions of a revered political figure within the party that the subject obviously dislikes, I get consistent opposition despite the fact that the actions and positions have no common ideological glue. And of course, I always tailor the questions towards the person based on our preceding discussion. The point is not to sway them on any actual positions, but rather to hold up a mirror and show them what they've become—a party hack with an enormous bias.

While I utilized several disconnected decisions of President Obama for the Republican questionnaire, I could have just as well used disconnected actions of former President Bush for a third liberal questionnaire and gotten the same results. The fun part always comes when I ask people to ponder the probability that they disagree with every single thing this person has done, especially considering that the issues are completely unrelated. This usually forces their mind to work way harder than it had anticipated when they awoke that morning.

The exercises lead us to a logical question: How can so many people fall into such broad based and predictable patterns of political thinking? To get the truth, we must start at the very origins of one's political beliefs. In this chapter we will explore the nexus which facilitates political polarization; that between the two party system and basic human psychological tendencies.

American Political Psychology 101

People usually become politically active because of a passion for one or a few issues. It could be gun rights or it could be gay rights. When you become passionate about an issue you become politically active. Regardless of whether your political activity is significant such as local activism or insignificant such as reading politically oriented columns and articles, you naturally start to engage people and sources of information that are like minded on the issue.

Because every national political issue in our society is neatly divided between two parties, you end up being increasingly exposed to one set of views or the other. The acute nature of the two party system and concurrent American political spectrum results in people defining themselves over time as one OR the other. That is two political parties derived from two broad ideologies for an infinite number of highly complex issues and policies. Momentum truly matters, as a strong opinion on one national issue will beget another.

As this process unfolds, you get closer and closer to being a hard-core believer, possibly culminating *with a provocative bumper sticker on your car* (which identifies either who you are or says something negative about your perceived opponent). This is because you repeatedly engage the same individuals and even the same sources of information for political discourse. A worldview develops over time and before you know it you are taking on and defending views that weren't yours to begin with.

Those who originally wanted low taxes are now pro-life and vice-versa. Those who were originally pro-gay marriage are now against drilling for oil in Alaska and vice versa. Because you are increasingly exposed to one side you increasingly hear one-sided arguments that are often rhetorical in nature or even absent of all the relevant facts. For these reasons, those with the *partisan sickness*** become

** definition: a condition in which the patient has a prepackaged negative judgment of any and all actions of the members of the opposing political party; often resulting in unpleasant dinner party conversations, emotional arguments, and a higher than normal usage rate of the terms 'fascist' or 'communist' (currently being substituted with 'racist' or 'socialist').

defined by their automatic nonoccurrence with any and all actions of the other side.

If you are from a politically oriented family you needn't even go through the previously described process of political discovery, as your parents will raise you to think one way or the other. If this is the case, the self-discovery process usually to be had, if any, is rebellion against those views passed down from your family (and often against one's childhood altogether). In cases such as these where the next generation does not buy wholesale into their parent's political beliefs, he/she usually ends up believing the complete opposite—*because it was really all lies you see.*

Regardless of where you end up, there is a psychological aspect to the processes of political polarization, and it is related to how your mind interprets and remembers concepts. Surely someone has told you to make a great first impression because it's always the most important. Why do we always say this? It is more than just a casual saying; there is a lot of truth to it.

Think about this hypothetical situation: Bill gets a new job. He then pulls off a fantastic performance on his first project. But then, he has a series of blunders that turn out less than favorable for the company. However, Bill's boss's perceptions were formed by that first great performance. Therefore, Bill's boss's mind is resistant to change its view of Bill as a worker. The reverse would have been true if Bill's first project turned out to be a disaster but those thereafter turned out pretty good. It would be harder for Bill's boss to perceive him as a good worker because of that bad first impression.

Once you have an impression of someone or something, it becomes difficult to break that original thought pattern. In Psychology of Intelligence Analysis, Richard Heuer explains that memories are believed to be stored in the brain as connections between neurons that make patterns.[1] So essentially, all of your memories and beliefs take the form of almost mental paintings.[2] Once these mental paintings are formed, they are extremely hard to change and even become self perpetuating.[3]

1 Heuer, Richards J. Psychology of Intelligence Analysis, Center for the Study of Intelligence, Central Intelligence Agency, 1999; pgs 17-25. Known hereafter as "Heuer, Psychology…". Public domain.
2 Heuer, Psychology…, pgs 17-25.
3 Heuer, Psychology…, pgs 17-25.

To highlight this Heuer utilizes a few simple but effective illustrations to show how difficult it is to change the way you see something once your perceptions are formed—including that presented below.[4]

Look at the below drawing[5] and tell me what you see? You can actually see this image in two very different ways, but it is much harder to get your brain to see it the other way once you have made up your mind:

Please skip to one of the following bolded sections depending on what you see:

1) **If you see a young woman:** Look at the tip of her chin and her ear. Now force your mind to see her chin and jaw as a big nose and her ear as an eye. Also see her necklace as a mouth. The young woman became an old woman!
2) **If you see an old woman:** Look at the tip of her nose and then her eye. Now force your mind to her see her eye as an ear with the tip of her nose as a chin.

---

4 Heuer, Psychology…, pg 12 .

5 Original U.S. copyright of image prior to January 21, 1923; public domain.

Regardless of how you first saw the image, notice how your mind keeps returning you to your original impression. Political views are no different—once they form they are extraordinarily resistant to change.** This leads to a particularly acute form of *confirmation bias* that we call *political bias*. Confirmation bias is defined as, "... a type of selective thinking whereby one tends to notice and to look for what confirms one's beliefs, and to ignore, not look for, or undervalue the relevance of what contradicts one's beliefs".[6]

Referring back to the previously provided fictitious story of Bill the office worker: You have your image of his competence or lack thereof formulated based on his initial performance. Now however, imagine those close to you repeating on a daily basis how great he is. Then imagine that you turn to your news channel, newspaper, or blog of choice and all of the stories are presented in a manner that not only make Bill look good, but his detractors seem wrong, stupid, or even evil. Once your political views are formulated, this essentially surmises the situation in contemporary America, as people surround themselves with individuals and sources of information that are like minded. The political thought process becomes like a self-licking ice cream cone as everything you consume simply re-enforces your worldview, which in turn serves as an impetus to go out and find more likeminded sources of information.

Political biases are also more severe than standard biases because they are so much more important to the individual. Unless you actively touted how great Bill the office worker was, you didn't care when he fell flat on his face. In politics however, emotions play an especially strong role because once you articulate your views you feel as if you have a vested interest in their defense. This is not to mention that those infected

---

** While this is an extremely superficial discussion of psychology, you can get Heuer's book here: http://www.amazon.com/Psychology-Intelligence-Analysis-Richards-Heuer/dp/1594546797/ref=sr_1_1?ie=UTF8&s=books&qid=1268273518&sr=1-1. Check out page 11 for a series of images entitled, "Impressions resist change". Heuer's book was actually written for Intelligence Officers within the federal government. They are tasked with interpreting raw data and then conveying their analysis to senior decision makers. For them, the onset of a strong bias in favor of an incorrect assessment can lead to strategic intelligence failure. I was struck by the applicability of Heuer's discussion to things so much broader than just intelligence analysis. In essence, you can almost pretend his material was written for political analysis and take away just as much. The image above, My Wife and My Mother-in-Law dates back to an old German postcard circa 1888, but was adopted by cartoonist W. E. Hill in 1915.

6 The Skeptic's Dictionary, http://skepdic.com/confirmbias.html, last accessed on May 2, 2009.

with the partisan sickness believe the other side is not only interfering with their lives, but actually ruining the country.

Biases form all the time... Your old relative tells you things were better in the 1950's and your father swears one pizza place is better than another even though he won't go anywhere else. Political biases however, rise to a level above and beyond nostalgic memories or inconsequential personal preferences. This is why you don't fight as hard over which pizza place is best or which decade America's greatest. The decisions to be made within the realm of politics will in some way touch your life and those of your children, and therefore are deeply personal.

The hallmark of a confirmation bias is when one only looks for what confirms his or her beliefs and ignores that which does not. And henceforth many Democrats believe that conservative de-regulation policies under former President Bush enabled the banks to over lend, resulting in the mortgage crises. Many Republicans think the same industry was mandated, under the auspices of former President Clinton to amend lending practices in order to expand home ownership amongst the poor. This of course led to many people owning homes they couldn't afford.

Actually, in the editorial entitled "Reagan Did It", Left Wing *New York Times* columnist Paul Krugman doesn't even waste his time with the already down and out former President Bush, he decides to go after the conservative Holy Grail by blaming the entire crises on Ronald Reagan![7] Right Wing columnist Ann Coulter does a great job convincing her readers that the crisis is the result of political correctness forcing banks to loosen their criteria for lending.[8]

They're both either intentionally misleading their readers or are actually convinced that the other political party is completely at fault for the crises. Neither side takes into account what the other side is using as their strongest evidence to support their arguments. As a reader and regardless of your political views, you should be extremely skeptical of any commentator who so blatantly doesn't even address the full argument of the other side.

I'd have to guess they're both knowingly misleading their readerships—who are by extent simply incorporating what supports their own

---

7 Krugman, Paul. *Reagan Did It*, New York Times online, May 31, 2009. http://www.nytimes.com/2009/06/01/opinion/01krugman.html?_r=1&partner=rssnyt&emc=rss, last accessed July 15, 2009.

8 Coulter, Ann. They Gave Your Mortgage to a Less Qualified Minority, http://www.anncoulter.com/cgi-local/printer_friendly.cgi?article=275, last accessed on July 15, 2009.

views while ignoring that which does not (to be found by reading the other side's easily accessible information). This is confirmation bias defined. I encourage you to read these pieces.*

Choosing Your Political Lens...

Now that I've made my political choice, I'm here to pick up the lens through which I'll view any and all political issues from now on!

The tendencies to simplify and categorize broad complex societal issues act as enablers for political polarization and bias...

The natural human tendencies to simplify and categorize assist in the process of political polarization as you incorporate different policies, decisions, and even things into your default view of the political world.

---

* They can be found here:
http://www.nytimes.com/2009/06/01/opinion/01krugman.html?_r=1&partner=rssnyt&emc=rss
http://www.anncoulter.com/cgi-local/printer_friendly.cgi?article=275

In addition to the mind's tendency towards the formation of biases, we also have a great tendency to oversimplify that which we do not understand. Not unlike how your mind wrestled with whether the image was an old woman or a young one, the mind wants answers on matters of state and governance (i.e. 'politics').

Except unlike whether Bill the office worker is competent or incompetent or whether you see an old woman as opposed to a young one, the societal issues to be settled by politics are infinitely more complicated. Too complicated in fact for most individuals to recognize unless they are actually in a related profession (such as a doctor struggling to serve his or her patients in the current health care system or an engineer working on strategic missile defense) or have devoted significant time and energy towards understanding the issue.

But most minds don't take these things into account and instead choose to make sweeping generalizations about why social security will fail or what is needed to wean us off of foreign oil. Simplification in the political context enables people to rationalize and accept the explanations given to them by their *partisan pundits* and politicians of choice. The two party system further exasperates this because we actually have squeezed every last political issue and policy into two broad categories.

This dumbing down of political issues has reached an all time high with the emergence of the *partisan industry,* as we now have an abundance of *partisan pundits* to sell policies by merely criticizing the opposition. Why answer difficult questions when you can simply demonize the only other opposition that exists?

How many times have you heard partisan rhetoric such as: "It's the fault of the Clinton Administration that 9/11 occurred". "The U.S. created Osama Bin Laden when it gave the Afghan mujahedeen aid to fight the Soviets". And again, this brings us back to more current issues: "The economic crisis is the fault of the Bush Administration; no it's the fault of the Clinton Administration".

Now don't get me wrong, many things can be directly attributed to individuals and administrations. I have no doubt that had Al Gore been elected we would not be talking about how light of a footprint we should leave in Iraq. Sometimes cause and effect is as straight as a laser. But in most cases in which we discuss national level politics, it is not. If it is a partisan pundit pointing the laser, it is almost certainly not. Yet the more complicated the issue the quicker the mind will jump at an opportunity to simplify it because it fools the thinker into believing they are in the know. Partisans feed off this tendency like vampires, and will often try and construct the most short, likeable, and memorable phrases to push their party's agenda.

Let me give you a hypothetical scenario to illustrate how broadly complex societal issues can be simplified for political purposes: President Obama has said that his administration will talk to the Iranians in order to get them to give up their nuclear program. This is a break from the Bush administration's policy of not talking (i.e. intimidating) to Iran in order to accomplish the same goal. If after two years of talking Iran tests a nuclear weapon, the conservative pundits are going to have a field day. They're going to say that Obama's policy was a failure, he's the new Neville Chamberlain (the British Prime Minister who proclaimed to have achieved "peace in our time" by acceding to Hitler's 1938 annexation of Czechoslovakia), and that 'liberalism' just put the entire planet in danger. The pundits will draw simple line between Obama's "failed" policy and Iran having attained a nuclear weapon; a classic example of simplified cause and effect in an extraordinarily complex environment (in this case one that is truly global).

But will it really be that simple? The answer is no, because this simplified explanation will have completely ignored the alternative: A preemptive strike against Iranian nuclear facilities, something the American people and world were unwilling to tolerate. But the politicians (and especially their little partisan hacks) will pray on your simplicity because it will be politically expedient. And of course, I'm sure those in the partisan industry aligned with the Democrats will come out with their own absurd political explanation for how this is actually George Bush's fault even though he will have been out of office at this point for years.

But the desire for understanding of such complex issues begs for simplification because as has been said, true understanding of the nuances of a given national situation requires more due diligence than simply reading one article or watching one broadcast. This is impractical for every last American on every issue. The best policy for the individual is to simply be honest when they don't know something—and to realize when partisan pundits are grossly simplifying for the sake of politics. Although we will talk about de-polarization later, try and catch yourself the next time you are about to make a statement about government policy that is generalized or simplified. How will you know if your statement is generalized or simplified? Easy, you won't actually know what you are talking about.

Apples are fruits, string beans are vegetables, free trade is conservative, and green energy is liberal... what?!

Just as our minds tends to hold onto the first perceptions we have and generalize about complex issues completely outside of our knowledge base, the categorization of different people, places, and things serves a natural purpose—a means for our minds to organize the world. Like hot and stove, cats and selfishness (if you're a cat lover that's fine, as long as you're not a man AND a cat lover), sushi and wasabi; categorization is necessary. *Otherwise you might eat your Dragon Roll with wet cement.*

Unlike many other subjective areas of life, the pre-categorization of all things political make a strong bias difficult to avoid, as mismatched positions and policies that are intellectually and morally inconsistent are all squeezed into two neatly packaged categories. In contemporary America these categorizations now go well beyond mere policy and into culture. This takes on rather amusing manifestations, as personalities and lifestyles are formed around the politically polarized mind.

Conservatives nebulously identify many things as "liberal". Liberals nebulously associate many of life's outcomes with "oppression" (which can be substituted with "inequality", which is the goal of those we call "conservatives"... who are the opposite of "liberals". "Liberal" means "open-minded". If you are "open-minded" then you are for "progress"... which makes you a "progressive". If you are against the goals of "progressives", then you are against "progress". I am a "progressive". You are against me. You are against progress!).

In essence, categorization allows those with the partisan sickness to arrange the world and their lives accordingly—except it is truly impossible to fit everything into such broad categories as political viewpoints—no less two of them.

Speaking on what he calls "clustering", Nassim Taleb states in The Black Swan that: "Categorizing is necessary for humans, but it becomes pathological when the category is seen as definitive, preventing people from considering the fuzziness of boundaries, let alone revising their categories".[9] In the political context, this enables people to accept the associations of gun rights with the rejection of gay marriage and gay rights with the rejection of gun rights.

For individuals with the *partisan sickness*, political association hardens and perpetuates their views (returning us to the previously mentioned

9 Taleb, Nassim Nicholas. *The Black Swan*. Random House 2007. Pg 15.

self licking ice cream cone). These loosely associated political concepts serve as evidence that one's machinations are based firmly in intellectual reality.

The natural tendencies to simplify and categorize sustain political polarization—as you incorporate different policies, decisions, and even things into your default view of the political parties and their ideologies. The partisans depicted are in the final, terminal stages of the partisan sickness (I'm 100% sure they both have bumper stickers).

Before we move onto the next section, I'm going to throw out a bunch of nebulous concepts often popularized or perceived as fitting into political categories... just for fun... (please read them out loud so can you realize how ridiculous our society has become—be sure to re-state the category prior to each item, switching back and forth between the two... it is more amusing that way). *Conservatives, pick up trucks... liberal, vegetarianism...*

Conservative	**Liberal**
Pick up trucks	vegetarianism
rifles	Yoga mat
Bible	open-minded
Patriotic	Hybrid
eat Bambi	pretend Bambi is a higher life form (okay so I made this last one up myself)

The two party system is extraordinary conducive to the described tendencies...

Although it has many benefits, the two-party system encourages political mis-categorization and simplification. This is because the leaders within it need only simplify and demonize the position taken by their sole opponent in order to galvanize public opinion. Simplification and extraordinarily generalized points of view have become default positions among the populace. If not attuned to it, simplification of even the most complex issues becomes extraordinarily difficult to avoid.

But to be fair to our fellow citizens and even ourselves (since I was a political hack before I unbrainwashed myself), the arrangement of the U.S. political system is especially conducive to the tendencies previously described. Our two party system ensures that every debate must fall within two viewpoints, thus acting as an enabler for the mind's tendency towards simplicity, entrenchment, and categorization. That's two viewpoints for issues in which there may be an infinite number of factors, any of which require extensive study to comprehensively understand.

Many Americans do not ponder how small our political spectrum really is—comprising of just Democrats and Republicans or more broadly liberals and conservatives.** It is also in the interests of not only the partisan industry but politicians to simplify the debate as much as possible.

** This book is not intended to be a call for a 3rd national party or even meant to be deliberately critical of the two party system, but rather to help the reader recognize their own political biases as well as those of others. It is a look (at times satirically so) at how the American public has become polarized, something I consider alarming and not good for the country. Your conclusions will be your own, but my hope is that people will become more critical in their thinking and less likely to accept every debate we have at face value.

It is also important to denote that traditionally, the narrowness of some of our debates could have been taken as a sign of prosperity. Our political system has always been stable and we've lacked extremism because generally speaking, things have been going pretty well.**

But alas, things have definitely taken a turn for the worse. The current state of debate in our country is not healthy, as the shrinking pool of non-polarized Americans scratch their heads in bewilderment as we swing from a Right Wing to a Left Wing government; all the while wondering where on earth they can go to get fair and honest news coverage.

I am not necessarily arguing against the two party system per se, but rather pointing out how easy it is to fall into clichés within that system. This leads to unhealthy debate, ideologically driven policies, and even hatred amongst our citizens. It is not good for our country and has clearly gotten out of control.

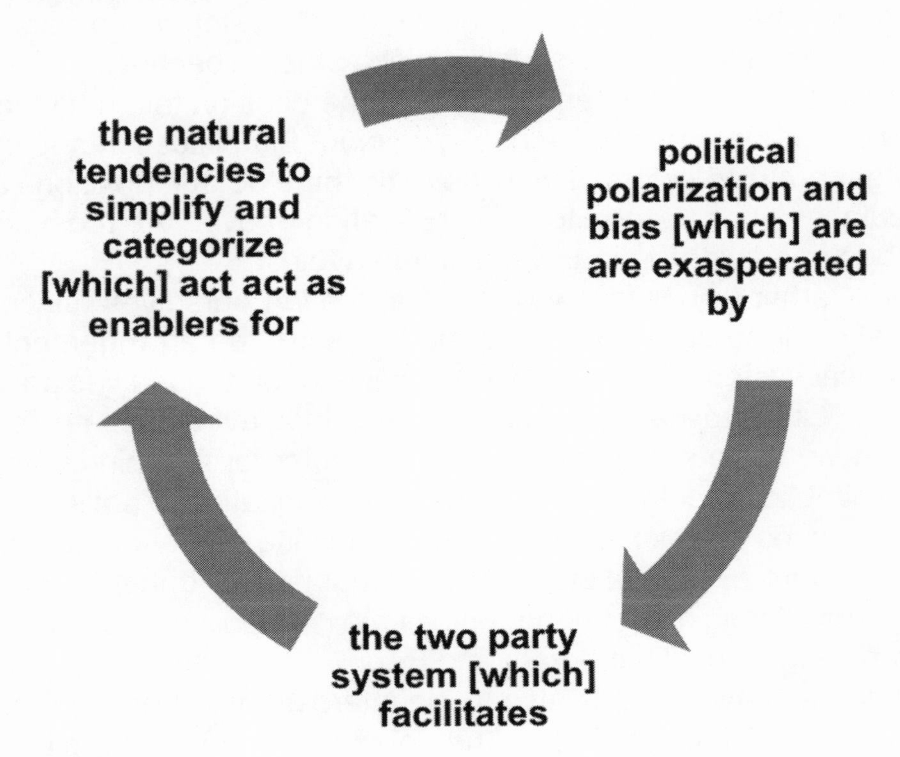

** In Parliamentary systems there inherently exist a much more diverse group of voices. In India for example, parliament is occupied by free market economists and straight up communists alike--but of course the communists have a constituency because so many people live in such destitute conditions. Parliamentary systems are also inherently more unstable--a choice against which was a deliberate one by our founding fathers.

Thus far we have examined our own political views in light of the nexus between the two party system and our natural psychological tendencies. Now we are going to explore something that's gotten really ugly. We're going to talk about the transformation of our media into a mighty *partisan industry*—much of which is now the ultimate arbiter of not just intellectual and moral inconsistency, but political polarization.

CHAPTER 3: The Rise of the Partisan Industry

The mainstream media perpetuates polarization by accepting the oversimplified analysis provided by politicized sources of information. It is oblivious to the partisan filter through which it so very often reports the news.

Before discussing the entrenchment of politicized information amongst what we traditionally considered to be the 'mainstream media', we must first make a distinction. For the most part there exist two types of news that perpetuate political polarization: There is the media that specifically comprises the partisan industry, and then there is the oblivious, or 'mainstream' media. The key difference is that the oblivious media inadvertently perpetuates partisan culture by accepting the simplified analysis provided by politicized sources of information. It does this because partisan analysis provides simple answers to complex questions. These questions otherwise require real expertise and research to truly answer.

The partisan industry on the other hand specifically seeks to profit by deceitfully selling political opinion in the form of news. This is done by presenting 'the news' in the form of shaped analysis, memorable sound bites, and above all, sensationalized political arguments.

In sum: I don't think all media is bias, but stupidity is a force to be reckoned with! As always however, there do exist shades of gray (which unfortunately seem to be shrinking).

Now I want you to please repeat after me:

THE MEDIA ARE NOT SUBJECT MATTER EXPERTS, THEY ARE JUST JOURNALISTS.

THE MEDIA ARE NOT SUBJECT MATTER EXPERTS, THEY ARE JUST JOURNALISTS.

THE MEDIA ARE NOT SUBJECT MATTER EXPERTS, THEY ARE JUST JOURNALISTS!

Mark my words: The people you are watching and reading every day often know just as much as you do about the given subject matter on which they are reporting, minus some peripheral digging and gluing together of facts and quotes. In fact they may know less, but are emboldened to make definitive statements due to status (i.e. in front of a camera on national television) and out of necessity (if they didn't tell you something you wouldn't listen).

Think about your own profession. Maybe you are a teacher, an astronomer, or a snow mobile racer/part time salmon fisherman. Think about how much more you know on that given topic than everyone else. This is because you work 40 hours a day, five days a week, and for years within that profession. You know and understand a level of detail about your profession that the average person could not fathom.

Yet those who report the news are responsible for discussing every single thing on the planet dubbed 'newsworthy'—i.e. any given topic on any given day. That which is truly 'newsworthy' usually entails a level of complexity that may even elude people knowledgeable about the subject. Think of the economy for example. How many economists or bankers really understood the systemic risk facing our banking system before it crashed in late '08? Not many.

People in the media face a daunting task: Talk and write about the topic of the day. Given how long it takes to truly become an expert on a topic, the only thing on which the media could be reporting on in which you should have total confidence is on the intricacies of reporting the news itself! I am not saying that news reporters are any dumber than a given sample of the population, but precisely the not-so-opposite (you should try not to generalize): They are just like everybody else! The sooner you realize this, the sooner you can begin to sanitize your informational input from superficial and especially politicized news.

This is why I am convinced the national media loves what I call *stupid news* (def: news that is easily digestible, impacts people's emotions, and usually should **not** be discussed on the national level**). The media LOVES stupid news perhaps even inadvertently, meaning it's not a conspiracy to distract you from the real issues as some political extremist standing on the street corner would have you believe (*It's the corporations... maaaaan!*).

The truth is actually a lot simpler than that. Stupid news is something that requires no effort on which to report since the media itself is comfortable talking about the topic. Examples of stupid news include how an old woman fended off a mugger in some remote part of Florida on MSNBC. This 'story' ran amidst one of the largest budget crises we've faced in decades—they even had the woman on for an interview! CNN did a report on how oversized handbags may hurt your back while Congress was negotiating the first stimulus package. Anything involving Brittany Spears, Beyonce, or Brangelina qualifies as stupid news. *Except coverage of their negotiating with Russia to place our missile defense radar in Azerbaijan as opposed to Poland.*

Occasionally there is a story that takes hold that is both stupid and national in character—usually amongst the most sensational. Remember the Y2K virus, that mythical bug that was supposed to impede the functioning of all computers at midnight on New Year's Eve? How about Africanized killer bees? Yep, I guess they're still coming.

** So what do I mean by something not being on the 'national level'? Am I being subjective? Absolutely NOT. A news venue that is national (not your local newspaper) should report and discuss issues that impact the nation; things that are 'strategic' in nature. In this context that means the issue has a structural impact on the way Americans live. Amazingly, even Congress gets involved sometimes in issues that are not truly national issues. Examples of this include Congress banning private ownership of primates and holding hearings on the use of steroids in professional baseball. Whenever I am watching the news and something that is not national (or qualifies as 'stupid') is discussed, I change the channel. With respect to Congress, I suspect it will continue to get involved in matters inconsequential to the nation until the people learn to make a basic distinction: Is this an issue with which Congress should be concerned? If it is not, send your Representative or Senator's office an e-mail telling them to get back to work!

If these things are so farcical, then why did the media report them? It is simple: The media did not have the expertise to question them and therefore is subject to manipulation, just like you and I. The daunting tasks facing media personal include what to report, what not to report, what is relevant, what is not relevant, and of course what is fact or not fact on every single issue.

Normally the media has a tough job. Now add politics into the mix. Whereas on a regular issue the media already has a tough time grasping, fact checking, and conveying the story; now it has to contend with a whole new category of sources from whom to get facts, quotes, analysis, and opinions.

Take global warming for example. Normally a scientific issue would be featured on the news in the form of an interview with a scientist or a feature on a new study from a University professor, etc. But because global warming has been elevated out of the realm of science and into the realm of politics, much of what we now hear on the subject is from *partisan pundits*; hardly those you want to listen to for information on ANY topic, no less one that requires an advanced degree to truly grasp. While occasionally someone with expertise in science is on television to explain the evidence vis-à-vis global warming, it now overwhelmingly partisan individuals who explain it in narrow, politicized terms.

On non-political issues the media CAN BE manipulated, even inadvertently by the source of the information (re: Y2K, killer bees, etc). On political issues the media IS manipulated, always by the source of the information. The problem is that on political issues the ultimate sources of the information have a vested or strong ideological interest in seeing one political party or the other come out on top—former advisors, partisan think tanks, ideologically leaning non-profits, etc.

The role of the non-partisan media in perpetuating political polarization lays with its accepting of narrow partisan explanations and arguments for why things are occurring (such as the economy crashing), why they're not occurring (such as the economy recovering), or why the sun is exploding ("its really George Bush's/President Obama's fault").

In other words, the oblivious media is exactly that because it is oblivious to the politicized lens through which it is increasingly reporting the news! Here is a fictitious example of how the media gets manipulated by politicized analysis:

Some far off country invades another one. Here in the U.S., some human rights groups begin to publish imagery of human rights violations committed by the attacker within the smaller, weaker country; which also happens to supply its region with 70% of its natural gas.

Due to the aforementioned issues, the potential American response quickly becomes a politicized issue here at home, with one party advocating one position and the other party advocating another (be it sanctions, sending flowers to the dictator of the invader, or all out war).

In addition to reporting the superficial facts of the story (the day, time, and weather conditions upon the invasion, etc), the media understandably looks to bring in experts on the topic to answer questions (the who, what, why, where, how, and whens). Except as the issue has now become politicized (with one political party accusing the other of being a warmonger and the other side alleging weakness), the experts now required to provide analysis are primarily *partisan pundits* vice substantive experts on the subject matter.

Unlike experts on the topics at hand (such as on how the war will unfold sans intervention, the cultural history of the two countries, etc), the political pundits simply use the opportunity to further their own political agenda. They appear before the country as 'commentators', 'panelists', and 'contributors'; providing the American people with dumbed down politicized rhetoric.

They make nebulous arguments linking the opposing political party to the events at hand. They dig up old sound bites in which members of the opposite party are seen coddling the dictator of the invading nation. Pretty soon people have bumper stickers on their cars crying for war, peace, or just denouncing the other political party for how it would have supported Hitler were he alive today.

My point is that partisan pundits do NOTHING CONSTRUCTIVE WHATSOEVER to help America actually understand the issue. Even worse, they do nothing to help America understand the risks of the policies they perpetuate. Yet they are the go-to experts for all things that broach the political barrier. Once an issue does so, they essentially own the spectrum of information.

Now let me give you a real life example of an oblivious news source filtering its information through a partisan pundit (i.e. 'political expert'). The other day I was watching a CNN 'report' on Congressional earmarks. The anchor threw out a few shallow facts about earmarks in bills signed by President Obama. He then asked "political contributor" James Carville for his take on the situation—is President Obama going back on his word? (The President campaigned on a platform of impeding the practice of earmarks).

Now I'll tell you right now that I do not consider CNN to be a really biased news station—and henceforth we're having this discussion in the 'oblivious' section of this chapter (you will see my assessment of where several major sources of news fall on the partisan spectrum in the next chapter). Nor did I detect any political ideology whatsoever from the anchor. Living up to the 1st definition of partisan pundit (re: *those who seek to comprehensively defend their political party, often at the expense of honest analysis, fact, and even country*), Carville offered the audience a four word (or so—I'm paraphrasing here) sentence in response to the question of whether President Obama went back on his word: "President Bush did it [too]" (with a disgusted look on his face).

This is partisan punditry at its worst. Although Carville was brought on for his "analysis" as a "contributor", all he did was use the opportunity to reassure constituents within his own party that President Obama's actions were just. His 'analysis' was essentially that Republican critics were being hypocritical because all of Bush's bills had earmarks as well. Let us not forget that President Obama campaigned on not tolerating earmarks. So there can be no doubt that earmarks, generally speaking (or at least as per President Obama's own words) are a questionable mechanism for getting things done in Congress.

But Carville cannot even tolerate a substantive discussion if and when a member of his own political party is right or wrong (or perhaps less rigidly, whether he can or cannot force Congress to follow his agenda) without referring to the opposition. Carville, like all partisan pundits cannot be trusted for sound analysis because he has a political agenda. He used one of the cheapest tactics possible: When in an untenable argument, divert attention to thy political enemy. It is difficult to even label what he said as an 'argument'. It was a cheap diversion at best.

One cannot be trusted for analysis when they automatically defend one political party on every issue. Again: What is the probability one agrees with every single thing that one party or the other stands for? Can there be a more succinct example of confirmation bias? Remember, confirmation bias entails including information that supports your beliefs while excluding that which does not. In this case Carville chooses to ignore something mildly critical of President Obama (arguably not even within his control) while incorporating negative information into the argument about former President Bush; thus re-enforcing a mental painting inside the minds of like-minded viewers.

You may be wondering at this point, what does this author really think about these issues? I mean, he has to have an opinion, right? My opinion is that we have to hold ourselves to a higher standard than simply demonizing the opposition when asked for analysis. Simply offering political rhetoric in place of educational analysis does nothing for our country. In fact, it may lower the intelligence of the viewer. The world is more complicated than us verses them, Democrat versus Republican, and liberal versus conservative.

Yet partisan pundits are so successful because they satiate your mind's desire for explanation—they trick you into thinking you know something by grossly simplifying the issue. The oblivious media turns to them simply because they require analysis on the issue at hand.

They also bring ratings. What do you think the average person is more inclined to watch: A Jerry Springer like version of the news or some drab historian explaining the history behind the aforementioned two fictitious countries at war? Sean Hannity berating someone from the left beats honest and in-depth analysis nine times out of ten. It is partly the mind's tendency towards simplification and partly because it is simply more fun. Are the proclivities toward simplicity and something called 'fun' one and the same? I don't know, but why make a categorization when you're not sure?

Before we turn to the real topic of discussion in this chapter, I will use one more real example of a story that appeared to be dramatically simple if taken solely for what was presented in the news. This is because partisan pundits not only took control of the debate, but the entire flow of information.

If you turned on any of the major networks during the debate of President Obama's tax plan you would have seen an amazingly narrow set of discussions—"There are earmarks in the bill!" "Taxes are going down for 95% of Americans!" "The deficit is unsustainable!" "A deficit is necessary during times of economic crises!" There was very little actual analysis of the substance of the bill (over 1,000 pages long!). If you are watching the news or a debate (often now one and the same) on a political issue, you need to ask yourself a simple question: Do I actually understand any of the complexities of this issue after taking in this information? It was entirely possible to follow the financial crises through a 24-hour cycle and not learn a damn thing. Yet it seemed as if the entire country had taken on one partisan pundit's sound bite or the other's to 'argue' the merits or demerits of the stimulus package.

The point in highlighting the media's frequent reporting of stupid news, shallow analysis, and an over reliance on partisan pundits is simply to draw your skepticism of what you consume. To be fair to any non-partisan media that is left out there, they have a tough job. What is important to the individual and the real point of what you just read is to acknowledge that if you only learn about something from the 'news', you don't truly understand the issue with any kind of depth. If you learn about anything political on the news and later find yourself about to make an opinionated statement, ask yourself: Am I about to generalize? Is this really true? Do I have any real facts to support what I am about to say? If so, and as we'll see in the next chapter, whose facts are they? Are they the only relevant facts? Be skeptical not just of what you hear, but what you think.**

Here is a fictitious example of how our depth of knowledge on any given issue progressively gets shallower as we move further away from the issue. The issue in this case is national energy policy.

<u>Expert</u>: "America's future lay with a wide composite of energy sources if we are to truly achieve energy independence. It will depend on our ability to better exploit renewable energies, continue research on clean coal, and even use nuclear power to plug the gap. If more hawkish peak oil theories prove correct, we may also need to drill while re-tooling our national energy infrastructure. Regardless, all sources have their draw-backs and all represent opportunities."

<u>The mainstream media</u>: "And in this next segment we will explore the prospects for renewable energies. Could they hold the key to America's future? According to some experts, yes. But critics say the technology simply isn't ready yet to replace fossil fuels. Proponents cite the five billion dollars some in Congress would like to dedicate towards pure research."

** Understand that I am not carte blanche bashing the entire profession of journalism, calling them all stupid, or any other such thing. That would only confirm the contention of the mind's tendency toward simplicity and generalization. It is quite natural that there should be a profession called journalism in which the world is kept abreast of developments. What I am saying, however, is that you should have no illusions as to how much you know on a given topic simply because you witnessed a discussion about it on TV.

Society Versus Depth of Knowledge

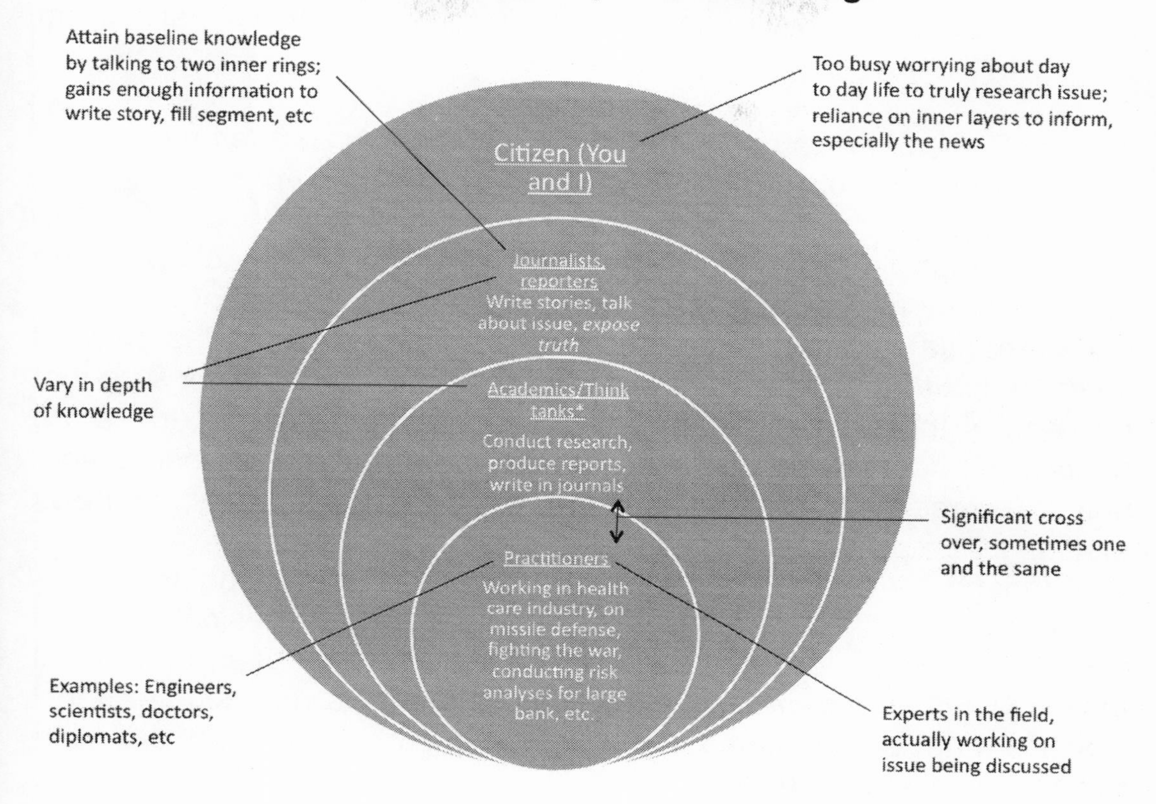

(To see an enlarged version of this graphic, please visit www.whatisbipolarnation/graphics.com)

As this is society relevant to a given national issue, notice how YOU are on the outer ring. This is not to demean the reader, as I, the author, am right there with you on 99% of issues. (Personally, the thing that I know above and beyond everything else is how little I actually know.) For the purposes of this chart, the two middle layers have a basic function: Educate/inform the majority who are not actually working on the issue at hand. The most inner layer actually provides the service, builds the product, conducts scientific testing, etc. The further from the center, the more superficial the understanding of the issue. Please note that the lack of distinction between non-bias sources of media and the *partisan industry* will be resolved at the end of the chapter.

The mainstream media filtering its output through partisan sources: "One senator is advocating nuclear power as a key component of America's future, but critics charge this could simply lead to more Chernobyl like disasters. Here with us now is the Executive Director of Greenpeace."

You: (Near the water cooler) ... and I'll tell ya', if we get more of these nuclear power plants we're gonna be eatin three eyed fish's that's all I'm sayin...".

The Partisan Industry on the other hand is not even attempting to inform, but to imprint a political point of view on your mind.

This brings us to the central topic of discussion in this chapter (the above was more or less a tirade against the obliviousness of our mainstream media). There has been a drastic change over the last several years in that to which we refer as "the news". Although I'm not sure that any one of these events or the nation's reactions to them caused the change per se, I can tell you that in the aftermath of the contested election of George W. Bush, 9/11, and the Iraq WMD controversy; the news media just simply wasn't the same.

Although I am in no way blaming it for the current bipolar character of our nation, I would definitely have to say that the single biggest catalyst for the collapse of our traditional media has been the ascent of Fox News as the industry leader. Fox's rise was probably the most significant development in the news since the development of the internet as a media platform.

It gained steam amongst not only conservatives but also the mainstream in the wake of 9/11 because its pundits so aptly captured the anger and despair we all felt. But perhaps not so aptly, it also provided the answers and blame we were so desperately seeking. Fox provided 'the news' in new formats—mostly through the lenses of commentators—but also in the form of opinion shows in which two or more guests would have yelling contests, the winner being determined by which guest provided the most numerous and entertaining anecdotes. Complementing Fox was the rise of politically leaning conservative websites such as drudgereport and breitbart.com.

But this is not about blame, it is about recognizing the problem. While I do believe that Fox's emergence allowed other, pre-existing biases on the left to come out more openly, the truth is that much of the rest of our national media was always bias and I do not hesitate to say that it did lean left as conservatives allege. Liberals act as if Fox News and Rush Limbaugh invented the concept of political bias itself. In reality, they simply elevated it to new levels. Levels in which the commentator just happens to ALWAYS support his/her political party of choice while disagreeing with the other.

Likewise I'm not sure what came first, polarized America or insanely biased media. But the fact is that we are now faced with a self-licking ice cream in which polarized America is providing a strong following for biased sources of news while biased sources of news are continuing the steady polarization of America.

Today we have an MSNBC that is a mirror image of Fox on the left. That is right. If you are a conservative and hate MSNBC, you are watching the exact same thing from the other side of the ideological spectrum. And as for liberals who hate Fox, stop accusing them of distortion and look at what your own ilk are doing. It is exactly the same. Media bias in contemporary America is like two wings of the same butterfly. They are now inseparable and doing grave harm, not just through politically shaping what you see but also in inciting outright hatred. Drudgereport not to your liking? Why not visit huffingtonpost on a daily basis? That's open mindedness for ya'.

Now I know that many conservatives and liberals will read this and argue that I am simply morally equivocating between the two networks. To this argument, I simply ask that you hold tight and wait until the end of the next chapter—as I will prove to you that the tactics of the partisan pundits on both of these networks are NO DIFFERENT!

In chapter two we discussed the formation of political biases, which are a form of confirmation bias. The hallmark of a confirmation bias is when someone only looks for what confirms her/his beliefs while ignoring that evidence which does not. Conservatives are now watching Fox News and listening to Rush Limbaugh while liberals are reading the New York Times and watching MSNBC (while still pretending that Fox News and Rush Limbaugh created the concept of political bias itself[10]).

Every minute America watches and listens its views become more entrenched—and hence less willing to compromise or reason with the other side. When you add it all together—the major networks (Fox and MSNBC), the major Newspapers (The New York Times, The Washington

---

10 This lay at the root of their desire to implement the Fairness Doctrine. They honestly believe that bias only exists amongst sources that cater to conservatives. Thank god the White House has specifically spoken out against its implementation.

Times, etc), radio (Rush Limbaugh, etc), and the internet/blogosphere (huffingtonpost.com, breitbart.com, etc); it is now easier than ever for Americans to re-confirm their biases on a daily basis. We are now spoon-feeding politicized information to enormous factions—both comprised of Americans—both think America would be better off without the other.

A mighty *partisan industry* has replaced what we traditionally call "the news", it is defined as: *those who seek to profit by selling a particular political point of view or ideology in a biased manner; usually accomplished through the emphasis of news and information that bolsters the preferred political point of view.***

Whereas the regular media unintentionally simplifies complex issues and accepts the analysis provided by partisan pundits at face value, the partisan industry isn't even trying to tell you the truth. The way it operates is rather simple. It plays to those tendencies described in chapter 2. The 'news' is presented in the form of shaped analysis, memorable sound bites, and above all grossly simplified partisan explanations for anything involving government, law, or policy. Because the news is presented in a much more entertaining and even understandable fashion (through over-simplification), there is no financial incentive to present it in a truly fair and balanced fashion.*

A new type of quasi celebrity has arisen with this industry. They are not doctors, they are not engineers, they are not scientists, nor are they legal experts. They are the new intellectual priests of our time who work within the partisan industry to sell ideology in a biased manner while enriching themselves. They gain a following by discussing political issues in an emotional and highly charged manner, rife with rhetorical remarks that have little relevance to actual policy. Oftentimes they even use comedy. Once they have you, they will never fail to re-enforce that mental painting of your political side as good and the other bad.

And thus, a partisan pundit is defined as: *one who seeks to comprehensively defend their political party, often at the expense of honest analysis, fact, and even country.* Def 2: *one who makes political arguments utilizing dishonest techniques of persuasion. These techniques often include: Simplification of the issue, demonization of their opponents*

** Definition created by author.

* This is NOT a plug for the so-called "Fairness Doctrine", so please do not read into this for more than what is actually stated. As we'll see in the next chapter, there is only one way to 'solve' the problem, and it most certainly does not involve bureaucrats.

*at the expense of analysis, an intentional reliance on the anecdotal in order to reach broad conclusions, or the intentional emphasis of some facts over others.***

Partisan punditry is now firmly entrenched within our culture—on television, radio, and in print. Walk into the book store today and you will see the shelves packed with faces on books that claim to 'expose' the other political party or reveal its deepest darkest secrets (*its leaders are trying to destroy America!*).

Outlook on the aforementioned self-licking ice cream cone...

The media's job is to seek explanation on behalf of the busy, hard working citizen who is too concerned with his or her daily life to become an expert on any given issue. But seeking the truth is difficult, especially when there is no accountability. It requires careful analysis through research and understanding (i.e. 'effort') to present information in a non-biased fashion.

Ideally our news reporters would be deep skeptics who loathe both political parties! As things stand now however, even the non-biased media is not up to the task of thoroughly informing the public because it is completely oblivious to the spectrum within which it reports politically related information—a spectrum now defined by two sets of partisan pundits. Partisan pundits cannot be trusted to give anything broaching an unvarnished opinion because they simply do not have the truth in mind.

Media bias and its impact upon our country is going to get worse. In the short term MSNBC and FOX will continue to lead the televised charge (as CNN pathetically attempts to re-invent itself as an issue driven network).[11] But truth be told, the entire future of the traditional "news" is in doubt. Not only is the future of the print medium for disseminating news at risk of extinction due to plummeting advertising revenues, but even the traditional model of television is going to face severe turbulence as its own business model faces the biggest threat it has ever known. Emerging in their places is a sort of 'Televisionnet' to which people are increasingly going to watch movies, shows, and get the news—at a fraction of the price! If not free...

** Definition created by author.

11 http://www.tvweek.com/news/2009/03/cnn_ratings_down_fox_msnbc_gro.php; last accessed August 10, 2009.

The positive aspect is there will be a greater number of sources from which to get the news. Because the internet is still in its infancy stages, it is also a sort of a wild west of innovation; we simply don't know what business model may soon arise. The negatives are twofold: 1) As the news fragments and multiplies, the quality of journalism may plummet. This is because there will be less of an incentive to do truly investigative journalism and instead just provide analysis. 2) People will increasingly split along ideological lines when choosing their sources of news. This will continue to amplify the political divide in our country even further as political biases (and even hatred of one another) become more entrenched.

Earlier in this chapter I presented a chart depicting society versus levels of depth on any given national level issue. While the average citizen, you and I, were on the outside of the chart relative to the given issue, the other layers represented those working on or attempting to inform us about the issue. The partisan industry was not included on that chart. And truth be told, it still should not be because it does not even seek to inform. It seeks to influence and shape. That is not the job of the news.

Although one cannot measure it in tangible terms, the partisan industry's impact on the political polarization of our society cannot be underestimated. For it is not just misleading us, it is actually making us dumber. As we now view every issue through two lenses—that of gross politicization and simplification. (Politicization + simplification = pundification)

And thus, lens really is a good word with which to describe the partisan industry. It sits firmly between the citizen and truth. Once you see the world through the lens that is the partisan industry, *the partisan sickness* is an all but certainty:

The Partisan Industry Versus Society

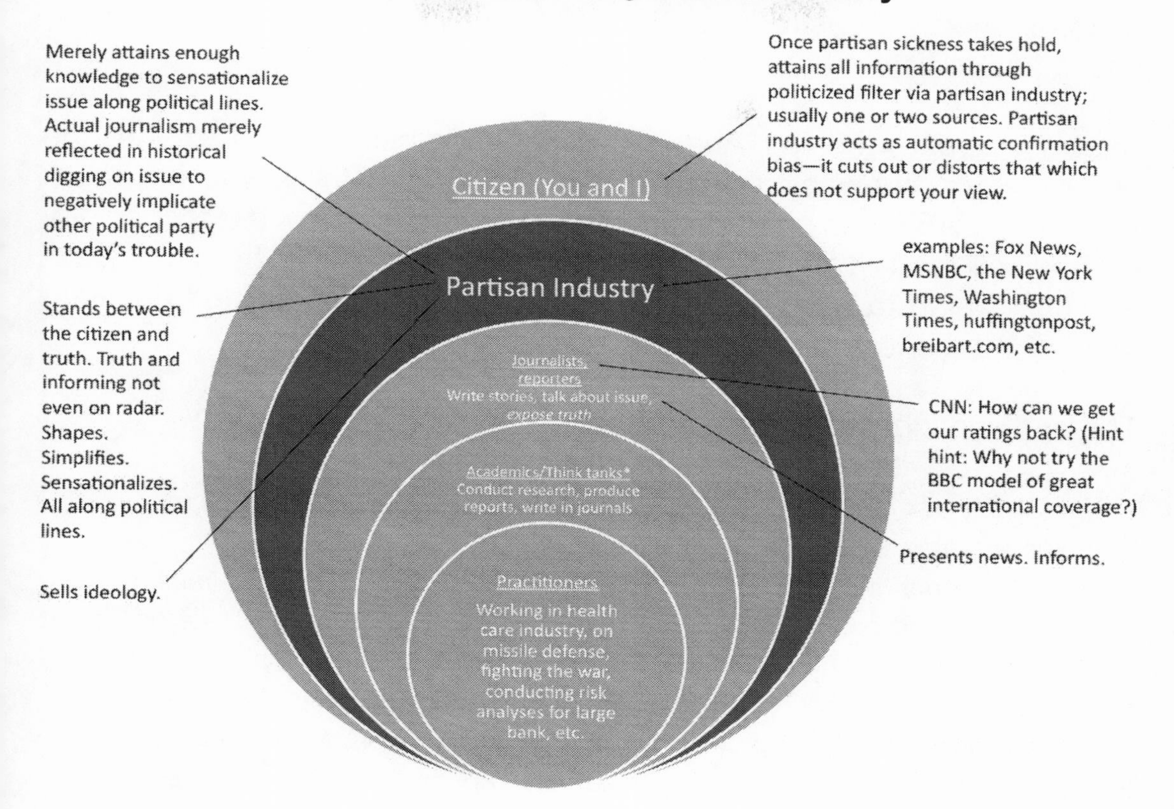

(To see an enlarged version of this graphic, please visit www.whatisbipolarnation/graphics.com)

Here is the same graphic presented earlier on society versus depth of knowledge on any given issue. Notice that the political industry is now included within the graphic—firmly between being truly informed and the citizen. If the inner layers all have the function of providing the rest of society with different levels of fidelity on the given issue, then the partisan industry really shouldn't even be on the chart. Its function is simply to make you see the issue a certain way. The truth is irrelevant.

Here is the same example provided earlier on levels of societal depth versus energy policy. This time notice how the partisan industry has been included.

Expert: "America's future lays with a wide composite of energy sources if we are to truly achieve energy independence. It will depend on our ability to better exploit renewable energies, continue research on clean coal, and even use nuclear power to plug the gap. If more hawkish peak oil theories prove correct, we may also need to drill while re-tooling our national energy infrastructure. Regardless, all sources have their drawbacks and all represent opportunities."

The mainstream media: "And in this next segment we will explore the prospects for renewable energies. Could they hold the key to America's future? According to some experts, yes. But critics say the technology simply isn't ready yet to replace fossil fuels. Meanwhile the administration has a plan to allocate five billion dollars for research and development of wind and solar power."

The partisan industry (liberal source):

> All this talk about offshore oil drilling and the price of gas and the pump is a bunch of BS. In fact, the Republican Party is colluding with the oil and gas industry to drive up the price of energy. This is criminal. The oil and gas industry, buoyed by their Right-Wing minions are on a coordinated and well-thought out mission to end the twenty-six year old moratorium on off-shore oil and gas drilling. The goal? To at once embarrass Barack Obama, take down the Congressional Democrats, increase corporate profit and further drive up the price of energy.[12]

The partisan industry (conservative source):

> … You could put all those stupid compact fluorescent light bulbs you can find in your house, it's not going to produce any more energy and it's not going to reduce the price of gasoline. And you can unplug your cell phone charger and your toaster and computer and whatever else. You could put solar panels on your lawn mower. You could put solar panels on your house. You could put solar panels on the roof of your hybrid; it isn't going to make gasoline any cheaper. You can put windmills wherever you don't want them. It ain't going to make gasoline any cheaper. There is no substitute for oil, and there isn't going to be any time soon. So this whole notion that we're not going to be able to lower the price any time soon by drilling, not gonna get lower prices right now, nothing else that the people are proposing will do so, either…

---

12 "The Right-Wing Offshore Drilling Scam", http://www.dailykos.com/storyonly/2008/6/18/134047/614/81/537906; last accessed August 12, 2009.

> Barack Obama and the Democrat Party are out there suggesting that drilling for oil off the coastline of the United States and at ANWR is nothing more than "the failed policies of the past." Can I be honest with you and tell you what the failed policies of the past are? In 1988, New York governor Mario Cuomo shut down a nuclear plant. That is a failed policy of the past. In 1996, the delightful, the wonderful, the roguish Bill Clinton vetoed exploration and drilling in ANWR. That is a failed policy of the past. Both of those are failed policies of the past. Changing from these failed policies of the past would be to un-fail the failures, to dis-fail the failures. Building nuclear plants, opening ANWR -- and then we could sue Cuomo and Clinton for malpractice, political malpractice, for gumming up the works...[13]

You (with conservative partisan sickness): "The Democrats care more about the environment than the American people!"

You (with liberal partisan sickness): "The Republicans don't even represent the American people, they represent the corporations."

---

13 http://www.rushlimbaugh.com/home/daily/site_061808/content/01125108.guest.html; last accessed August 12, 2009.

CHAPTER 4: The Art of Partisan Punditry

The systemic solution to the partisan industry lay with the individual. An intellectual war is being waged upon America that will be won, unless the citizen is able to recognize and defeat the methodologies of the biased.

They train our young to criticize America, not celebrate it. **They** welcome condoms into the classroom but ban God and the Ten Commandments. **They** encourage tolerance for the teachings of the Koran but not for the teachings of Jesus Christ. **They** oppose the Pledge of Allegiance, tell us that 'God is dead,' that 'Christianity is for losers,' and that evangelical and Catholic conservatives are more dangerous than radical Islamic militants. **They** tell us that fuel-burning SUVs are bad for America, but flag-burning SOBs aren't [bolded emphases added by author]

—Sean Hannity on the *true* agenda of the left, Let Freedom Ring.[14]

---

14 Sean Hannity, Let Freedom Ring: Winning the War of Liberty over Liberalism, HarperCollins Publishers, February 2004.

... the insurance industry owns the **Republican Party**. Not exclusively. Pharma owns part of it, too. Hospitals and HMO's, another part. Nursing homes, they have a share. **You name a Republican, any Republican**, and he is literally brought to you by campaign donations from the health sector. [bolded emphases added by author]

—Keith Olbermann on what is *really* driving opposition to Democratic plans for health care reform, August 3, 2009.[15]

It isn't taxes and it isn't tea parties and it isn't stimuli[s] and it isn't Sotomayor and it isn't health care reform and it isn't the public option. **Do some of these people** simply fear and hate a black president? [bolded emphasis added by author]

—Keith Olbermann on why conservatives *really* oppose the President's policies, August 7, 2009.[16]

The leader of genius must have the ability to make different opponents appear as if they belonged to the **one category**; for weak and wavering natures among a leader's following may easily begin to be dubious about the justice of their own cause if they have to face different enemies. **As soon as the vacillating masses find themselves facing an opposition that is made up of different groups of enemies their sense of objectivity will be aroused and they will ask how is it that all the others can be in the wrong and they themselves, and their movement, alone in the right**. [bolded emphases added by author]

–An unidentified historical figure (for now)

I made a very pointed statement in the last chapter: The liberal and conservative partisan industries are roughly equivalent. It doesn't matter who is in sum more right or more wrong. The crux of the issue is that their tactics are exactly the same and therefore cannot be trusted on ANY issue. This is because their presentation of those issues is deeply biased. If you consistently watch one over the other, you should be alarmed not just by what you are seeing, *but by what you are not*.

---

15 http://www.msnbc.msn.com/id/32284299/ns/msnbc_tv-countdown_with_keith_olbermann/; last accessed August 15, 2009.

16 http://www.msnbc.msn.com/id/32330236/; last accessed August 15, 2009.

But now, I'm going to prove it to you. To make a statement is one thing, but to demonstrate it is another. It truly is my hope that if you consistently watch Fox, MSNBC, read the New York Times or Washington Times that you'll pay attention here, because it is you who needs to understand the art of influence more than any other. And it is us—together—who need to help our fellow Americans on both sides of the political spectrum understand the true nature of political bias.

But first a detour: I recently came across a very interesting story. Famous news anchor Dan Rather went on a very public tangent about the destruction of the media as he once knew it. Not completely dissimilar to what I told you in the last chapter, Rather stated rather (pardon the pun) succinctly that: "Corporate and political influence on newsrooms, along with the conflation of news and entertainment, has created the dumbing down and sleazing up of what we see on the news."[17] Obviously I couldn't agree more. It was his solution however, that was so confounding:

> I personally encourage the President to establish a White House commission on public media... The free press, as established by the First Amendment to the Constitution, ought to operate as a public trust, not solely as a money-making endeavor... it's time the government make an effort to ensure the survival of the free press. [If not the government] then an organization like the Carnegie Foundation should take it on... If we do nothing more than stand back and hope that innovation alone will solve this crisis... then our best-trained journalists will lose their jobs.[18]

Although he by no means specified what a "public trust" would actually entail, one would think that such an institution would not differ dramatically in purpose from The Fairness Doctrine. The Fairness Doctrine is described as "... a policy of the United States Federal Communications Commission (FCC) that required the holders of broadcast licenses both to present controversial issues of public importance and to do so in a manner that was (in the Commission's view) honest, equitable, and balanced."[19]

---

17 Aspen Daily News Online, http://www.aspendailynews.com/section/home/135834, last accessed on July 30th 2008.

18 Aspen Daily News Online, http://www.aspendailynews.com/section/home/135834, last accessed on July 30th 2008.

19 http://www.fairnessdoctrine.com/; last accessed on August 16, 2009.

While Mr. Rather hit the nail on the head that is the partisan industry with his statement on political influence and entertainment, I find it pretty amazing that he could offer such a solution without realizing the inherent dangers of taking the news away from several large corporations (not to mention countless bloggers and websites) and in essence putting it into the hands of one giant corporation we refer to as "the government".

Shortly thereafter the Federal Trade Commission announced a workshop on journalism entitled: "From Town Criers to Bloggers: How Will Journalism Survive the Internet Age?"[20] Although no precise topics of discussion or goals were announced at the time, the statement of the FTC Chairman which accompanied the announcement did not give me too much hope: "Competition among news organizations involves more than just price."[21] And thus, he was insinuating that journalism should function on the behalf of something beyond profit. Keep in mind that the mission of his organization is "...to prevent fraud, deception, and unfair business practices in the marketplace."[22]

And make no mistake about it there certainly is fraud and deception in the market place. But the problem with the media is that you are not buying a tangible good that clearly works (as advertised) or doesn't, such as a widget (oh the irony); you are buying ideas and information. And therein lays the very problem with a governmental—or 'systemic' solution.

Were something akin to the Fairness Doctrine be implemented, it would be impossible to enforce. This is due to the inevitable clash between what those in power deem to be "honest, equitable, and balanced", as opposed to those in the media and public Because such terms are so subjective in the realm of ideas, I can think of no governmental solution that will solve the problem without itself posing an infinitely greater danger to society. While the output of the partisan industry is abysmal, I would choose it and whatever the consequences in place of the government regulation of ideas and information.

It's good that others are sensitized to the problem. But the inevitable question facing us now is: What can be done? First a recap: As per the conclusion of the previous chapter, the problem is going to get worse as the sources from which people get news continue to fracture on the web

20 http://www.nytimes.com/2009/08/24/business/media/24ftc.html?_r=1; last accessed August 27, 2008.

21 http://www.nytimes.com/2009/08/24/business/media/24ftc.html?_r=1; last accessed August 27, 2008.

22 http://www.ftc.gov/bcp/index.shtml; last accessed August 27, 2009.

while further merging with politicized entertainment. At this point in time the incentives to present truly professional, non-politicized news simply aren't there. MSNBC's pulling into the #2 spot ahead of CNN and second only to Fox is surely indicative of things to come.[23] (Although CNN has of course brought it on itself by presenting some of the most brainless information available—weekend programming aside). The future of the hardcopy newspaper and magazine as formats are in doubt, likely to be a memory by 2025. Replacing them? An army of more partisan, blog-like online publications.

Is all lost? Absolutely not. The news industry is going through upheaval due to the nexus of technological change and emergence of the partisan industry. Innovation may still show us the way out of this crisis, as the internet is still in its infancy stages and there are bound to be many unemployed, truly professional journalists.

Regardless and as always, American discourse will only return to 'normal' commensurate with the citizen's understanding of what it is they're actually seeing. It is up to us to not only understand how the politically biased operate, but to declare war on their kind. That's right, war, of the intellectual sort. We must not only understand the true nature of political bias in the media, but confront those with the partisan sickness in a constructive manner. We need a revolution against the status quo, but revolutions always start at the bottom.

First we understand how the partisan industry operates and then we confront both sides in a measured, respectful tone. The goal is never to start fights, it is always to change society for the better. Change starts in the mind—at first in the individual and eventually amongst the collective.

The Art of Partisan Punditry

There's a reason why political bias in the media has become so prevalent. It has become so prevalent because it is so cunning. When people think of "political bias", they automatically categorize the results as "lies." The logic goes something like this: *If someone is politically biased, then they lie!*

Yet very rarely do biased commentators, columnists, or media organizations outright lie. Lies are exposed rather easily, forcing the organization

---

23 http://tvbythenumbers.com/2009/06/30/msnbc-beats-cnn-in-prime-for-quarter-first-time-ever/21649; last accessed August 16, 2009.

responsible to issue a retraction (or at a minimum being called out by another organization). Political bias is infinitely more difficult to wrap one's head around. You can watch the partisan pundits on MSNBC or Fox News for an entire evening, walk away vehemently agreeing with their worldview and not have actually heard one single lie. And hence, millions are able to do so every day and remain oblivious to the methods with which they are manipulated.

You see, lying is drilled into our heads from a very early age precisely because the concept is so easy to understand—it can even be taught to a child. Yet there exists so much that is equivalent to lying about which we do not maintain the same level of vigilance. So ask yourself: How is it possible that liberal or conservative partisan pundits can talk about the same issue, lead their viewers to take diametrically opposite positions, and yet neither one of them outright lied to do so?**

They are able to do so because their methods defy simple categorization. When something defies categorization it is difficult for the human mind to understand. Let me give you an example of a partisan tactic that would be used by the politically biased and not fall into this category—it would be easy to identify.

'Source selection' would probably be highlighted by any work on bias in the media. If you cherry pick your sources of fact or analysis from the likeminded (such as right leaning think tanks or left leaning professors), the story will naturally become that which you want it to. This is a tactic that would not be too difficult to understand, so as long as the basic purpose or track record of the source is clear.

However, what those in the partisan industry do is so much more than this. *To say that they select their sources would be akin to saying there is a drop of water in the ocean*. And while one can easily distinguish between a multitude of narrowly defined tactics, such an exercise is unnecessary. It would simply overload the average consumer with information; thus preventing them from seeing the big picture and most importantly, concisely conveying to others what it is the partisan industry actually does.

As I became a student of the partisan industry in preparation for this book, I have attempted to categorize (possibly to my detriment) its methods of persuasion. In doing so, I have narrowed it down to only three, they include the following:

** Yes, occasionally they do outright lie, but this by no means represents the vast majority of the time.

Political cherry picking

Political cherry picking is the most prevalent form of political bias. Cherry picking is defined as "the behavior of selecting only the data that confirm the preferred conclusion, [while] ignoring data that contradict it. Cherry picking refers to the *deliberate* exclusion of contrary cases."[24] Note that cherry picking is a deliberate act, whereas unconscious exclusion of data is the result of a confirmation bias.

In the context of the partisan industry—since nobody can possibly believe those we see on television and read in print to be so aloof—political cherry picking can be defined as "the deliberate selection of data that supports the preferred ideology, while ignoring or refuting that which undermines it."** This manifests itself as the comprehensive choice of not just angles and facts, but of the stories themselves; all in a manner that makes one political ideology seem preferable to the other. While it is perfectly legitimate to report any one story or fact that may make one party look good as opposed to the other, political cherry picking lacks subtlety once you're attuned to it. Amongst the organizations comprising the partisan industry, it is comprehensive in nature vice attributable to the occasional imbalance.

For example, liberal partisan industry will highlight instances of white on black hate crimes. Conservative partisan industry will highlight instances of black on white hate crimes. Liberal partisan industry will highlight corporations destroying the environment in pursuit of profit. Conservative partisan industry will highlight liberals destroying corporations in pursuit of the environment.

If a partisan pundit's political party is trying to sell a policy or piece of legislation, expect them to cherry pick which aspects of the legislation to sell. Expect them to cherry pick which of their opponent's arguments to refute. In fact, expect them to focus solely on that which is weak, blatantly wrong, or coming from the most detested members of the other side.

For example, why actually waste your time doing research to inform the public how much the average family's expenses will go up as a result of health care reform when you can simply state that said reform will result in "death panels"? On the contrary, why refute the legitimate grievances of those opposed to the reform when you can simply state that all

---

24 Definition from SkepticWiki, http://skepticwiki.org/index.php/Cherry-Picking; last accessed April 8, 2010. Emphasis of *deliberate* added by author.

** Definition created by author.

opposition is misinformed or ill intentioned (while highlighting and elevating the "death panels" comment)?

For any of the aforementioned stories you can expect partisan pundits to interview and cite sources that make their party's ideology seem favorable—and hence the reason why I stated earlier that to say they select their sources is akin to saying there is a drop of water in the ocean. What they do is so much more comprehensive. Ironically, this comprehensiveness renders most consumers oblivious to what it is they're actually doing. The bias is woven into the reporting on every level.

The goal of political cherry picking is simple: By choosing the ground on which they will fight at all levels of any debate, it becomes impossible for the audience to view partisan pundits as wrong. By continuously showing that audience what supports one worldview while ignoring or aggressively refuting the other, the partisan industry acts as an automatic confirmation bias on a societal scale. It is at worst lying by omission, and extremely difficult to detect for most consumers.

Sensationalized Political Demonization

One could argue that choosing to persistently focus on the ills and misdeeds of the opposition is simply a subcategory of political cherry picking. It is, to the extent that any instance of sensationalized political demonization could be a part of a broader politically cherry picked information set. But nevertheless it has become such a prominent feature of the partisan landscape (including within the back and forth between everyday partisan sickness infected citizens), that it warrants its own discussion.

To sensationalize can be defined as something like "to cast and present in a manner intended to arouse strong interest, especially through inclusion of exaggerated or lurid details."[25] Or even better: "to cause (events, especially in newspaper reports) to seem more vivid, shocking, etc., than they really are."[26] Demonization can be defined as "to represent as evil or diabolic."[27]

---

25 The Free Dictionary, http://www.thefreedictionary.com/sensationalize; last accessed April 15, 2010. Definitions from the Free Dictionary reprinted with permission from Farlex, Inc.
26 The Free Dictionary, http://www.thefreedictionary.com/sensationalize; last accessed April 15, 2010.
27 The Free Dictionary, http://www.thefreedictionary.com/demonization; last accessed April 15, 2010.

Therefore, sensationalized *political* demonization can be defined as: "to cast and represent the political opposition in the worst possible manner, i.e. ill-informed or even evil. This is usually accomplished through the exaggeration or embellishment of unfavorable associations, public gaffes, scandals, policy failures or instances of ideological hypocrisy."**

Essentially, partisan pundits use any and every opportunity possible to shape their audience's mind in opposition to the other political party. If the U.S. suffers a foreign policy setback, they'll blame it on the policies of the other party. If the U.S. suffers a setback vis-à-vis domestic policy, they'll blame it on the policies of the other party. If the U.S. suffers an economic setback, expect them to pull out all stops to make you truly believe it is the fault of the other party! (*While completely ignoring up to trillions of other data points*). The embellishment—or concoction—of historical instances of poor policy making by the other party in connection to present day ills exponentially strengthens the political narrative that has been so carefully crafted for the hyper partisan masses.

Whenever the opposition is caught in an untenable political position, such as an individual member in a scandal or an instance of policy failure, expect partisan pundits to make the anecdotal appear as the norm through repetition and elevation. They'll even let more important stories fall by the way side in order to do so.

When partisans are in an untenable political argument, expect them to simply go on the offensive—attacking the opposition. This is the political equivalent of the "he hit me first" argument. For example: Was it wrong for the Democrats to use 'reconciliation' to pass health care reform? Simple: *The Republicans used it 'X' amount of times during the past 10 years!* Was it wrong for the Republicans to drive up the deficit when they were in power? Simple: *The Democrats always ran a deficit!* By highlighting and elevating an anecdotal or current-policy-irrelevant instance of wrongdoing by the other party, partisans are able to make the opposition's argument seem hypocritical or disingenuous. It is one of the most effective methods of sensationalized political demonization because it not only redirects outrage, but also enables the partisan to avoid answering for his party's obvious inadequacies.

Perhaps one of the most prevalent examples of sensationalized political demonization is that alluded to with the last quote in the beginning of this chapter. It is the consistent casting of the opposite political party in the broadest, most generalized terms possible. By making their followers

** Definition created by author.

believe that all opposition to their policies fit into one at best misinformed and at worst evil category, partisan pundits derive multiple benefits.

The narrative that the entire opposition is nothing but leftists, fascists, communists, racists, socialists, corporate interests, etc; facilitates the myth that it lacks valid opinions or criticisms. A concurrent benefit is the creation of a false dichotomy amongst those with the partisan sickness (a false dichotomy is the illusion that there only exist two choices when there are in fact more). This false dichotomy is that there solely exist two political choices: Between one political party that only occasionally transgresses its purported ideology, and another that is so misguided it will simply destroy America. In other words, it radically strengthens cohesion within the group.

The goal of the partisan industry in its relentless employment of sensationalized political demonization is not to simply sway public opinion on any single issue or policy. It is to pathologically ingrain their follower's hatred of the opposition. The benefit of such pathology is that their following will continue to defend the party line no matter how much its actions blatantly contradict its purported values; they will simply see no alternative. Sensationalized political demonization makes defeat of the opposition's intellectual argument unnecessary.

Persistent use of Political Rhetoric

Essentially, rhetoric is a means of persuasive communication. A rhetorical device is "a use of language that creates a literary effect (but often without regard for literal significance)."[28] In other words the speaker or writer is being persuasive, but what they are stating actually has little or no tangible value. And thus, political rhetoric can be defined as "language that creates a political effect, but without regard for relevance or applicability to actual policy."**

Would any one example of sensationalized political demonization merely be an example of political rhetoric? Most likely, just like any use of political rhetoric or sensationalized political demonization may be examples of political cherry picking (it would depend upon on the proportionality of what's being reported in consequence to one political ideology as opposed to the other). However, while much of sensationalized political

---

28 The Free Dictionary, http://www.thefreedictionary.com/rhetorical+device; last accessed April 19, 2010.

** Definition created by author.

demonization will be rhetorical in nature, the majority of political rhetoric will not be sensationalized political demonization.

If what you are hearing is too generalized to prove false, impossible to retort with facts or just extremely catchy, it is most likely political rhetoric. If comedy or irony is being employed to make a political point, I can guarantee you it is political rhetoric. It may sound great, it may convey your feelings exactly; but does it actually mean something in tangible terms relevant to the issue at hand?

Political rhetoric not only fools the consumer into believing they actually understand the issue, but it provides the partisan on the street the very ammunition with which the larger political battle is fought. Whoever throws out the most numerous, short, witty, and digestible political rhetoric will win.

There are several benefits of relying on this type of speech instead of prudent analysis:

1) Political rhetoric is too general to prove false. For example, if the political party of your disdain advocates talking to a potential foreign adversary of the United States, you can simply retort: "They would have talked to Hitler were he alive today?!" If the political party of your disdain is advocating against the imposition of carbon restrictions on American industry (to in turn combat global warming), you can simply retort: "Do these guys even believe in science?!"

Note that both retorts fail to actually address the policies in question. They even fail to present an alternative. They are substance less jibes. Whilst an average citizen with the partisan sickness may unknowingly state such things as a matter of standard discourse due to their lack of substantive knowledge, the partisan pundit does so because it is the easy way to garner ratings while being impossible to prove wrong. Remember, these people have a staff and researchers at their disposal. Given their positions in society, they are undoubtedly brilliant and should therefore never be given the benefit of the doubt (the benefit being that they are simply unaware of what it is they're doing).

2) Witty and emotionalized oratory entangles the minds of the audience. And of course it does this at the expense of facts, ground truth, and intellectual argument. It renders them unable to rationally assess whether the argument is valid because it is in fact completely inapplicable to policy in the first place. The use of comedy or irony is especially powerful when

attacking the opposition. The average mind works something like this: *If it is funny or witty it can't possibly be untrue*!

3) It enables partisan pundits to become what they are in the first place. This is because political rhetoric is a cover for an inescapable truth: Even the smartest human being who ever lived only understood a fraction of a fraction of how the world works. Yet partisan pundits by their very nature must convince their audience that they are all-knowing vis-à-vis any and every issue that broaches the political barrier. In fact, the ratio of political rhetoric in one's arguments is inversely proportional to their depth of knowledge on the given topic.

Political Rhetoric Versus Depth of Knowledge

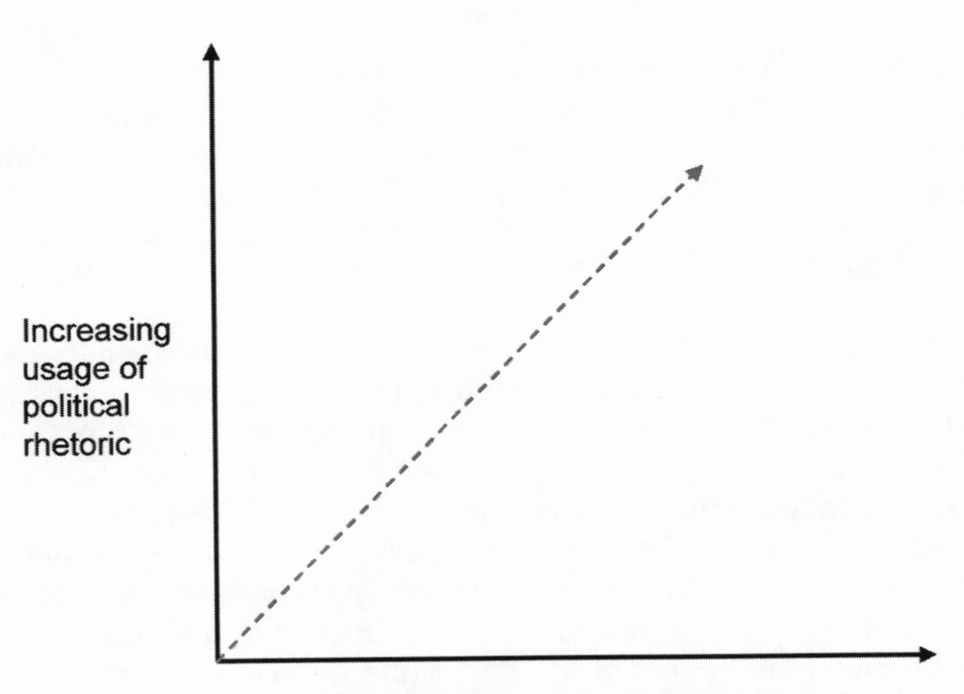

This is because a true subject matter expert, such as on health care or jet-pack propulsion for example, would never have the need to generalize or fool an audience into thinking a certain way through witty or comedic oratory. Perhaps saddest of all, true subject matter experts would probably bore the audience into submission, and henceforth the stunning success of partisan pundits. For these reasons—anywhere in between inability to speak with authority and lack of want due to concern over ratings—partisan pundits don't spend too much time engaging in legitimate debate or finding the most non-politicized experts to whom they can pose questions for their shows or columns. Such behavior would only give credence to the other side, bore their audience, result in low ratings, and by extension limit their book sales.

Political rhetoric detection: *An anti-body that combats the partisan sickness:* Whereas political cherry picking and sensationalized political demonization are easy to distinguish once you're aware of their existence, spotting political rhetoric is a bit less clear-cut. Being able to do so is a skill that falls under the category of "logic." It primarily comprises the ability to differentiate. The ability to do so is essential in mitigating the effects of partisan pundits and building outright immunity to the partisan sickness.

For these reasons we're going to do an exercise. Here is an excerpt from a July 26, 2009 editorial on the influence of the Blue Dog Democrats on health care reform. It is from Left Wing partisan pundit AND New York Times columnist (surprise, surprise) Paul Krugman.[29] Can you spot the political rhetoric?

> Reform, if it happens, will rest on four main pillars: regulation, mandates, subsidies and competition.
>
> By regulation I mean the nationwide imposition of rules that would prevent insurance companies from denying coverage based on your medical history, or dropping your coverage when you get sick. This would stop insurers from gaming the system by covering only healthy people.
>
> On the other side, individuals would also be prevented from gaming the system: Americans would be required to buy insurance even if they're currently healthy, rather than signing up only when they need care. And all but the smallest businesses would be required either to provide their employees with insurance, or to pay fees that help cover the cost of subsidies—subsidies that would make insurance affordable for lower-income American families.
>
> Finally, there would be a public option: A government-run insurance plan competing with private insurers, which would help hold down costs.

---

29 www.nytimes.com/2009/07/27/opinion/27krugman.html; last accessed on September 12, 2009.

> The subsidy portion of health reform would cost around a trillion dollars over the next decade. In all the plans currently on the table, this expense would be offset with a combination of cost savings elsewhere and additional taxes, so that there would be no overall effect on the federal deficit.
>
> So what are the objections of the Blue Dogs?
>
> Well, they talk a lot about fiscal responsibility, which basically boils down to worrying about the cost of those subsidies. And it's tempting to stop right there, and cry foul. After all, where were those concerns about fiscal responsibility back in 2001, when most conservative Democrats voted enthusiastically for that year's big Bush tax cut—a tax cut that added $1.35 trillion to the deficit?
>
> But it's actually much worse than that—because even as they complain about the plan's cost, the Blue Dogs are making demands that would greatly increase that cost.
>
> There has been a lot of publicity about Blue Dog opposition to the public option, and rightly so: A plan without a public option to hold down insurance premiums would cost taxpayers more than a plan with such an option…[30]

This is a great case because it so aptly demonstrates that it is not always clear whether or not something is indeed political rhetoric. If it were as simple as black and white, partisan pundits would not use rhetorical devices to sway your opinion. And thus it is truly debatable where this editorial delved into the rhetorical. The following statement certainly caught my attention: "… In all the plans currently on the table, this expense would be offset with a combination of cost savings elsewhere and additional taxes, *so that there would be no overall effect on the federal deficit…*".[31**]

It is debatable whether this is rhetoric because there is no way anyone can possibly know—even now that reform has been passed—whether any of the plans that were on the table, no-less the one that was passed—would or will have had an "no overall" effect on the deficit. This is especially true given that several key financial provisions within

30 www.nytimes.com/2009/07/27/opinion/27krugman.html; last accessed on September 12, 2009.

31 www.nytimes.com/2009/07/27/opinion/27krugman.html; last accessed on September 12, 2009.

** Italicized emphasis added by author.

the bill that did pass, such as taxes on certain health care plans, will not kick in for several years. Because we don't know if this will really happen, the statement is a generalization about the future that cannot be proven wrong or right. Therefore, it is actually unknowable whether or not it is political rhetoric because quite simply, we won't know if it was for years to come! Coming from a partisan pundit who was strongly supporting reform, he was at a minimum trying to convince the audience of his point of view by claiming an unknown factor in his favor.

Regardless of the verdict on that specific portion of the editorial, I would argue that even getting to such a point of active debate within your own mind as to whether something is indeed 'political rhetoric' means you understand the concept and are thus less susceptible to the partisan sickness. While an easy answer will at times prove elusive, your active mental wrestling over such categorizations almost guarantees immunity.

I'm going to vote no. That was not political rhetoric—he may just be wrong… or right depending on whether or not certain provisions ever do go into effect… but then again he did ignore the fact that nobody can truly know whether the bill will be deficit neutral… hmmm.

Regardless, the following was most certainly rhetoric: "… And it's tempting to stop right there, and cry foul. *After all, where were those concerns about fiscal responsibility back in 2001, when most conservative Democrats voted enthusiastically for that year's big Bush tax cut — a tax cut that added $1.35 trillion to the deficit?*"[32]**

Were conservative Democrats somehow wrong for worrying about the deficit because their past policies were said to have contributed to the current one (in an indirect manner no less)? Are all deficits created equal? Do two wrongs make a right?

The implication is that their voting on past tax cuts is mutually exclusive to present day concerns over the deficit. (*If you increased the deficit in the past, you cannot be against it today!*) The intention was to simply make the Blue Dog Democrats look hypocritical—and thus was an attempt to get the audience to dismiss the legitimacy of their concerns outright. Sensationalized political demonization? I'd argue no, it wasn't "sensationalized." But it is clearly political rhetoric, i.e. intended to create a political effect without regard for relevance or applicability to actual policy (in this case health care reform).

---

32 www.nytimes.com/2009/07/27/opinion/27krugman.html; last accessed on September 12, 2009.

** Italicized emphasis added by author.

In the interest of being FAIR AND BALANCED, we will now look at an excerpt from a right wing partisan pundit. Here is a July 23, 2009 excerpt from Glenn Beck, also on health care reform:

> ... Could it be that Obama realizes the incomprehensible nightmare that reparations would present to the country, things like who would pay, how much? Do all whites pay? Even if they can prove their ancestors weren't slave owners, weren't even here at the time? Would Hispanics and Asians pay? If so, how? How much? Maybe just the rich white would pay, say another 9 or 10% surcharge. What the heck. They can afford it. They don't even work for their money. They've been handed everything. These people don't work. They wake up in the morning. They tell their servants, "James, go out and pluck me some cash from my magic fairy money tree in the yard. I say $2 or $3 million should be enough for today. And then get out of my sight, you nauseate me. You have the sniffles? Oh, we should exterminate you... See, these are the tricky questions. But then again, they have nothing to do with Obama's objection to reparations. Obama is against direct reparations for one reason. He doesn't ever want the victim card to be lost. In 2004 he wrote, "I fear that reparations would be an excuse for some to say we've paid our debt and then avoid the much harder work." What is the harder work? What is the harder work? You don't want the debt paid because you don't ever want the leverage gone. The debt can never be paid. Instead he has a better idea. Universal healthcare and that's just the beginning. That's only one piece. Universal healthcare...[33]

Can you spot the political rhetoric here? Ha! Trick question! The entire excerpt was political rhetoric! Glenn Beck was making the argument that President Obama's desire to reform health care was really a back door attempt to provide reparations for African Americans! Never mind that universal health care has become a de facto position amongst the left and that our health care system definitively requires reform on at least some level.

Whilst I have spent the bulk of this chapter trying to convince you that partisan pundits, regardless of ideology, adhere to the same basic methods of persuasion (thus making them morally equivalent regardless of where you stand); I will now prove it. The best way to do this was to

33 http://www.glennbeck.com/content/articles/article/198/28317/;

actually dissect transcripts from partisan pundit programming. After each excerpt, I will state which methodologies of persuasion were utilized. Aside from my choices of MSNBC and Fox News, the actual date and programming were more or less random. In other words, I didn't watch night after night and then select the programs that best supported the established methods. I merely turned on the television when I reached this point in the book. Having chosen *The Rachael Maddow Show* first, I opted to go with Fox programming from that same date.

The first program chosen was the August 19, 2009 episode of the *Rachel Maddow Show*, which is hosted by leftwing partisan pundit Rachel Maddow every weeknight on MSNBC at 9:00pm. Nearly every segment defended liberal policies, scorned Republicans, or something in between. The following descriptions are by no means comprehensive—as I tried to just get the highlights.

Her first segment featured Houston protestors who held a rally against the "Cap and Trade" legislation passed by the House of Representatives in June of 2009. The legislation, which was not yet law as of the time of this writing, seeks to put caps on the carbon output of American industry—thus reducing air pollution and fighting global warming.[34] Highlights from the segment were as follows:

> ... the rally was organized largely by the American Petroleum Institute [API], and the crowd consisted at least in part of oil company employees bused in specifically for the event... As we reported two days ago, an internal memo from the President of the API that was marked sensitive was obtained by Green Peace and given to reporters. In the memo, the API [admitted] to organizing rallies like this. The memo asked oil companies who are members of the API to commit to their own employees attending these rallies... to deliver a quote "loud message to members of Congress", and to put a "*human face*" on the issue...[35**]

Maddow then provided another example of a corporation encouraging grass roots opposition to health care reform. The segment featured a group called unitedforhealthreform.com, which according to Maddow is actually affiliated with an organization called the United Health Group. Maddow then informed the viewer that the United Health Group is the

---

34 http://www.epa.gov/captrade/captrade-101.html; last accessed August 21, 2009.
35 http://www.msnbc.msn.com/id/26315908/#32484953
** Italics added by author to denote sarcastic tone.

second largest health insurer in the country, which is "[36]most famous for its connection to the Lewin Group." She then highlighted the frequent citation by Republican leaders of studies done by the Lewin Group on the pitfalls of health insurance reform. According to her, these studies are "...providing the anti-health reform talking points for health care."[37] The viewer was then treated to several clips of Republican politicians citing studies from the Lewin Group.

Breakdown: All opposition to Cap and Trade legislation as well as health care reform are acting solely on behalf of corporate interests. **Bottom Line**: Instead of actually presenting and then refuting their arguments, Maddow instead attempts to get the audience to dismiss them out of hand. The best way to do so is to politically demonize in a sensational manner through unfavorable associations and malevolent categorization.

In the next segment, Maddow informed the viewer that some of the organizations associated with an anti-big government, anti-tax rally that had taken place in Houston were also involved with a rally set to take place in Washington D.C. on September 12, 2009. She sarcastically described it as an "... *anti-tax, anti-big government, anti-special interests march on Washington*...[a] *citizen uprising*... [an] *against the man movement*...".[38]** She then commented on the "*fine print*" on the sponsoring organization's website (www.912dc.org):

> The fine print on this one? It is quite literally financial fine print. *This anti-tax, anti-big government, anti-special interests march on Washington, this citizen uprising, this against-the-man-movement is being organized and run by, oh, Freedom Works*... and non-profit Freedom Works has just hiked up the amount of money that it's charging organizations to take part in this grass roots march. So if you want to distribute your groups materials at the march, that used to cost a low-low price of $2500, now that'll be $10,000... $10,000 will also buy your organization a speaking role at the march. *Which is after all very free-markety!* Freedom Works says it is just trying to offset costs for stuff like stages and equipment... but charging $10,000 to take part in a grass roots march?[39]**

---

36 http://www.msnbc.msn.com/id/26315908/#32484953
37 http://www.msnbc.msn.com/id/26315908/#32484953
38 http://www.msnbc.msn.com/id/26315908/#32484953
** Italicized emphasis added by author to denote sarcastic tone.
39 http://www.msnbc.msn.com/id/26315908/#32484953
** Italicized emphasis added by author to denote sarcastic tone.

Maddow then provided her analytical bottom line: "When the press reports on these events, to assess their political importance, what politicians [need to] consider [is] the message for them from these types of rallies... trust me, the most interesting stuff is in the fine print."[40] She then had Senator Bernie Sanders provide commentary. He is an Independent and self-proclaimed 'Democratic Socialist'—meaning he is left of most Democrats.

Breakdown: The anti-tax protest was somehow hypocritical for charging other organizations to officially participate. **Bottom Line**: The entire segment was political rhetoric, as it had no relevance to any of the policies in question. The true nature of the organization and rally were not even a topic of discussion. Instead, the viewer was treated to sarcastic jibes such as Maddow's referring to the rallies as a "*citizen uprising*"[41] and "*against the man movement.*"[42]

Why does the organization charge for official participation? Is this a standard practice? These questions weren't considered because the segment was merely intended to create a political effect without any regard for relevance.

The next segment was on individuals who showed up to separate political rally totting guns. This rally was in opposition, and physically close proximity to a speech being given by President Obama. Maddow informed the audience that the organizer of these individuals is actually linked to a militia group that once conspired to attack U.S. government buildings. Mr. Frank Rich, an op-ed columnist from the New York Times, then came on to further discuss the issue in light of an editorial he wrote on the subject ("The Guns of August").[43]

Maddow asked Rich if he was concerned that President Obama might be assassinated. Rich responded:

> ... it began during the campaign [for the Presidency] where people were shouting treason and worse about Obama at Palin rallies, and essentially no one in the Republican Party that would condemn it. There were people you know sort of appearing in Nazi regalia and all the rest of it... and it's just been stepping up ever since then...[44]

40 http://www.msnbc.msn.com/id/26315908/#32484953
41 http://www.msnbc.msn.com/id/26315908/#32484953
42 http://www.msnbc.msn.com/id/26315908/#32484953
43 http://www.nytimes.com/2009/08/23/opinion/23rich.html?_r=1; last accessed on August 23, 2009.
44 http://www.msnbc.msn.com/id/26315908/#32484953

Maddow then asked Mr. Rich what citizens and the media could do to change the tone of the political debate. Mr. Rich responded that:

> I think we all have a role to play and I also think that politicians have a role to play. And it's shocking to me that very few Republican leaders have really condemned this kind of activity. In fact they've sort of encouraged it… well it's the 2nd amendment right and so on. Where does that get us? While I have the same faith you do in the people who protect us. The Holocaust Museum was not some obscure little backwater, it was a very… understandably well protected site in the center of Washington DC, and an eighty something year old man could go in there and create havoc and commit murder.[45] [Author's note: The Holocaust Museum was attacked by an 88 year old white supremacist on June 10, 2009[46]]

Mr. Rich then explained that in light of Palin's infamous "*death panel*" comments, health care reform has become

> … a proxy for everything they don't like about the government, everything they don't like about a liberal leaning administration, everything they don't like about change and that's another thing that's going on now… not just the Obama brand of change, we're going through this economic turmoil. People are frightened. Manufacturing industries have collapsed, my own industry is sort of half collapsed, people are sort of on edge anyway…[47]

Breakdown: The Republican Party is merely representative of the gun totting protestors and even the Holocaust Museum shooter. **Bottom Line**: While the viewer was initially made aware of a perfectly legitimate news story—that individuals showed up in close proximity to a Presidential speech with firearms; the item was merely used to sensationally demonize the Republicans. This was accomplished through a completely embellished association.

The next segment did not feature a political topic, but the one thereafter was dedicated to Republican Senator John Ensign's public apology

---

45 http://www.msnbc.msn.com/id/26315908/#32484953

46 http://www.cnn.com/2009/CRIME/06/10/museum.shooting/index.html; last accessed on August 22, 2009.

47 http://www.msnbc.msn.com/id/26315908/#32484953

for his affair with one of his staffers. The headline of the segment read "*Johnny Be Bad*" (on MSNBC's website the headline read "*Ensign Forgives Self*"), and started with Maddow joking at the fact that Ensign gave his original apology "*... standing in front of a public restroom sign...*".[48**] Maddow then explained that Senator
Ensign is hypocritical because:

> ... he had railed against Bill Clinton and against Senator Larry Craig of Idaho for when each of those men was called out for sexual indiscretions... back in 1998 as Kenneth Starr was alleging that President Clinton committed perjury then Representative John Ensign had a different perspective, calling for President Clinton to resign... a call for President Clinton's resignation based on the effect of his actions. What he had 'put the country through'. And of course his credibility. It's worth nothing that Senator Ensign's original confession left out lots and lots and lots of really tawdry details, verging on, even maybe not very legal details. Like the job he gave to his mistress' son at the Republican Party, and the money that his mom and dad paid to his mistress and her family after it was all said and done. But according to Senator Ensign today, resignation is still not on the table for him because quote: "I have not done anything legally wrong.[49]

Breakdown: Senator John Ensign is a hypocrite. **Bottom Line:** This was NOT an example of sensationalized political demonization because quite frankly, Maddow was right. That said the segment was rife with political rhetoric, such as the joke that Senator Ensign had given his original apology "standing in front of a bathroom sign."[50] Trivial jokes such as this were merely intended to embarrass the Senator but had no real relevance to the story whatsoever.

The fifth segment was on the U.S. government's Cash-For-Clunkers Program, which gave people up to $4500 if they traded in old vehicles that met low emissions standards in order to purchase more fuel-efficient ones (most Republicans opposed the program).[51] The segment began as follows:

---

48 http://www.msnbc.msn.com/id/26315908/#32484953

** Italicized emphasis added by author to denote sarcasm.

49 http://www.msnbc.msn.com/id/26315908/#32484953

50 http://www.msnbc.msn.com/id/26315908/#32484953

51 http://www.usatoday.com/money/autos/2009-05-11-chrysler-gm-cash-clunkers_N.htm; last accessed on August 21, 2009.

> We now turn to that *horrible, rotten, terrible cash for clunkers program, which continues to ruin everything for people who hate government programs that work really well and are very popular!* General motors has announced that Cash for Clunkers has increased sales so much for its vehicles that its boosting production by sixty thousand cars… in order to boost that production GM is rehiring 1,350 GM workers in North America. Somewhere in the anti-government corners of American politics, someone is trying to figure out a bumper sticker ready slogan to try and make that news sound like bad news. Good luck![52]**

Breakdown: Those who opposed the program were wrong because General Motors hired 1,350 workers. Bottom Line: The entire segment was political rhetoric because it was intended to have a political effect but was completely irrelevant to the actual policy in question. Maddow projected sarcasm, then provided the viewer a fact, and then projected more sarcasm. She did not mention ANY of the substantive arguments of the opposition.

The next segment was completely unrelated to U.S. politics, but was followed by one dedicated to mocking Senator Max Baucus for a verbal gaffe in which he stated that several protestors who showed up to a town hall on health care reform had "*youtubes*." Amidst a comically edited video presentation of Senator Baucus' tacit admission that he did not understand what youtube is, the viewer was treated to two similar gaffes by former President Bush and former Alaska Senator Ted Stevens; both of whom are Republicans who left office under unfavorable terms.

The "Pop Culturalist" who narrated the segment started off by saying: "Montana Senator Max Baucus*, whose conservative, bi-partisan, 'blue-doggery' hands the health care reform bill rests faced noisy protestors at a conference in* [unintelligible] *last week.* Senator Baucus told the New York Times: "There were a couple of people in the crowd with youtubes." *Yeah. Youtubesss.*"[53]**

Breakdown: Max Baucus is somehow unintelligent or disconnected because he didn't know what youtube was. **Bottom Line:** Repeatedly playing his verbal gaffe alongside those of former President Bush and former Alaska Senator Ted Stevens is an example of sensationalized

---

52 http://www.msnbc.msn.com/id/26315908/#32484953

** Italicized emphasis added by author to denote sarcastic tone.

53 http://www.msnbc.msn.com/id/26315908/#32484953

** Italicized emphasis added by author to denote sarcastic tone.

political demonization as well as good old political rhetoric. The segment created a political effect by leading the viewer to believe Senator Baucus is somehow unintelligent, but with no regard for any policy whatsoever. Even more so, it insinuated that he is equivalent to two highly unfavorable political individuals; especially to MSNBC's audience.

You may be asking why Max Baucus, a Democrat, was being sensationally demonized this way. Look no further than his introduction by the "Pop Culturalist." Max Baucus became the enemy to the Leftwing Partisan Industry throughout much of 2009 because he was seen as impeding health care reform in its most ideologically pure form—with a public option. This is a great but sad example of what happens to independent thinkers in post partisan industry America: You get cannibalized by your own for going down your own road.

Again and in the interest of being FAIR AND BALANCED, we will now scrutinize what was seen by the other half of America on August 19, 2009. The program chosen was "Hannity's America", which is hosted by rightwing partisan pundit Sean Hannity every weeknight on Fox News at 9:00pm (and hence we have perfect political symmetry!). Predictably, nearly every segment either defended conservative policies, scorned Democrats, or something in between. The following descriptions are by no means comprehensive—as I tried to just get the highlights.**

The first segment was dedicated to a speech given by President Obama in which he announced cuts to defense spending. The speech was made before the "Veterans of Foreign Wars." The viewer was shown a segment of the speech in which the President stated that "... to protect jobs back home building things we don't need, has a cost that we can't afford... this waste would be unacceptable at any time, but at a time when we're fighting two wars and facing a serious deficit, its inexcusable...". Hannity then asked the viewer: "*... isn't the stimulus all about creating jobs at home by building things we don't need, isn't the whole premise that spending is stimulus... now I think I remember someone saying that very thing...*".**

The viewer was then treated to an older clip of the President arguing that stimulus and spending are one and the same. Hannity then summed up this contradiction by stating: "*Oh I get it, I guess that's only true when it*

** Any and all portions of the program utilized in this chapter are purely for critical purposes.

** Italics added by author to denote sarcastic tone.

comes to pointless domestic projects and uh skate parks, not our national defense".**

Breakdown: The President is a hypocrite (as well as weak on defense) since he was willing to cut defense spending to save money while at the same time arguing that other 'not-definitively-needed' spending is simply "stimulus." **Bottom Line:** While Hannity was certainly embellishing an instance of ideological hypocrisy and obviously trying to pain the President as weak on defense spending, I wouldn't quite label this sensationalized political demonization. That said, the entire segment was political rhetoric. It wasn't really explained to the viewer WHAT kind of defense spending was being cut or WHY. Therefore, the segment was simply intended to create a political effect without relevance to actual policy.

This was followed by a series of clips in which the President pledged to cut taxes for 95% of Americans. Hannity then asked the question: "*But does anyone actually believe him*?"** He then cited a Rasmussen survey indicating that 82% of Americans believe their taxes will either go up or stay the same. The backdrop during this segment was a picture of the President with the text: "*NOT THAT GULLIBLE.*"

Breakdown: This segment was intended to convince the viewer that the President is a liar and therefore the people don't trust him. **Bottom Line:** This was simply intended to create a political effect with an actual discussion of tax policy. Furthermore, the viewer was given hardly any information on the poll. For example, what questions and or statements were made during the polling process? The segment depicted the poll as if it was being asked specifically in light of President Obama's being in office. Was this the case? The viewer would never know unless they went to Rasmussen's website. The entire 'segment', if you can call it that, was political rhetoric.

Hannity then turned to the Cap and Trade Bill that had recently passed the House of Representatives (the legislation seeks to put caps on the carbon output of American industry—thus reducing air pollution and fighting global warming).[54] The segment featured former Democratic Colorado Senator Timothy Wirth's statement that: "The Republicans are right – it's a tax and cap bill – that's what it is because they are raising revenues to do all sorts of things." A short discussion ensued about how Cap and Trade would increase taxes.

** Italics added by author to denote sarcastic tone.

** Italic added by author to denote sarcastic tone.

54 http://www.epa.gov/captrade/captrade-101.html; last accessed August 21, 2009.

Breakdown: The segment was intended to make the Republicans look vindicated in their opposition to Cap and Trade since a Democrat was speaking out against the bill. **Bottom Line:** As there was little discussion about the actual intricacies of the bill, one can conclude the segment was merely intended to have a political effect without regard to the policy itself.

Hannity then discussed a series of town halls the President had on health care, which were apparently described by the White House as "a chance for President Obama to hear from the American people." Hannity then showed the viewer a pie chart depicting the ratio of President Obama's words to those of the audience at the town halls (no I am not making this up). The ratio was 9 to 1. Hannity then stated: "*Maybe when he [Obama] says he wants to go it alone, that's what he means.*"**

Breakdown: The President is arrogant and doesn't care what the American people think. **Bottom Line:** As this segment was again intended to create a political effect without regard for any actual policies, it was indeed political rhetoric.

Hannity also had a segment called "Conflict of Interest", in which he began by stating that

> Democrats like Barack Obama and Nancy Pelopsi have accused concerned citizens attending health care town halls of being funded by special interests... but now shocking details have been uncovered that reveal that the people actually profiting from this debate are in fact high profile members of their own party...

He then cited an investigation by Bloomberg News about an advertising firm called AKPD Message and Media, "... which has received $12 million to produce ads supporting the President's health care plan...". The viewer was then informed that David Axelrod, one of the President's senior advisors, used to run the company and was still owed $2 million. Hannity then stated that another advertising company called GMMB is "...cashing in on the health care debate as well..." and "...employs a number of former Obama strategists...".

Partisan Pundit Michelle Malkin, who wrote the book: <u>Culture of Corruption: Obama and His Team of Tax Cheats, Crooks, and Cronies</u>, then informed the viewer that these two advertising firms (AKPD and

---

** Italics added by author to denote sarcasm.

GMMB) are smearing the tea party and anti-health care reform movements. This led to a discussion about the potential for a 'health care co-ops' instead of a 'public option', in which Malkin stated that "...you can't trust this administration, you certainly can't trust the kind of astroturfing propagandists that are trying to sell it to us... and co-op may more properly be called co-opted." (Author's note: The term "astroturfing" refers to a situation where an organized political effort by a special interest group is disguised to appear as an organic, grassroots movement by the people).

Breakdown: The Obama administration is corrupt since its members are closely tied to advertising firms which were supporting administration policy via paid campaigns. **Bottom line:** This segment bordered on sensationalized political demonization because it exaggerated or embellished an unfavorable association—that between the administration and giant corporations. It also wasn't clear from where the actual money came to pay for these campaigns. Regardless, the segment rife with political rhetoric. There was no real discussion about the intricacies of healthcare reform, least of all the tangible difference between health care co-ops and a public option. But of course, Makin did find the time to label the administration "astroturfing propagandists."

Another segment was entitled: "Destruction of the Dollar." It began with Hannity stating the following:

> With America buried in debt and no end to the spending spree in sight, legendary business man Warren Buffet is sounding an alarm that politicians in Washington need to hear. In a New York Times op-ed Tuesday, Buffet wrote quote: "We do not want our country to evolve into the banana-republic economy... Congress must end the rise in debt to G.D.P [that's gross domestic product] ratio and keep our growth in obligations in line with our growth in resources.

Hannity then further discussed the issue with Stuart Varney from the Fox Business Network. Mr. Varney told the viewer that Buffet—who is an Obama supporter and billionaire investor—is telling the President that he must retreat from government spending: "... the unwritten thing in the Warrant Buffet piece, was you gotta be careful with this health reform, for a trillion dollars, we can't afford it...". Mr. Varney later compared Buffet's rebuke of spending to Walter Cronkite's rebuke of the Vietnam War—which is now seen as a historic turning point in the war.

Breakdown: Warren Buffet is a billionaire who actually supports President Obama. He is saying we must control the deficit. Health care reform will drive up the deficit. Warren Buffet is speaking out against health care reform! **Bottom Line:** Again we have a jab at health care reform with no real discussion of how it will increase the deficit. As this segment was merely intended to have a political effect with no real discussion of policy, it can be categorized as political rhetoric.

In Sum...

You may have noticed that out of the three broad tactics of partisan punditry introduced earlier, there is one that was left out during our post segment analysis: Political cherry picking. Why? *Because to point to any one of the given segments as an example of political cherry picking would be akin to saying there is a drop of water in the ocean!* Every issue, every guest, and every fact was deliberately selected to support the preferred ideology while disregarding or refuting that which undermines it. In sum, they merely show you the world they want you see.

Did Maddow, Hannity, or any of their guests outright lie during any of the segments? There were definitely connections drawn that were rather severe stretches of the truth, so much so that they are in essence the same thing. Examples include that drawn between the Republican Party and the shooting at the Holocaust Museum as well as that between the Obama administration and corruption on the basis of David Axelrod's former company running ads in favor of Administration policy. With opportunities for such embellishments and insinuations so abundant, outright lying is simply unnecessary.

Was Hannity or Maddow right on any of the issues discussed? Sure! But any one example of a partisan pundit being 'right' is easily lost amongst the politically cherry picked whole, not to mention that the presentation of every issue is skewed in the first place. And thus you must ask yourself if you're agreeing with the position of a partisan pundit on the basis of their analysis: What do I really know about the given issue?

The bottom line is that you cannot trust the output of the partisan industry and especially partisan pundits to educate you. That is simply not what they do. What they do is politically cherry pick, sensationally demonize, and speak in politically rhetorical sound bites; thus acting as an automatic confirmation bias on a societal scale. Once their political vision is firmly imprinted upon your mind, you will not even seek the truth about the opposition's positions, for they are at best misinformed and at worst evil. And thus, compromise becomes all but an impossibility, as we have so sadly seen.

> ***partisan pundit**: one who seeks to comprehensively defend their political party, often at the expense of honest analysis, fact, and even country. Def 2: one who makes political arguments utilizing dishonest techniques of persuasion...***

These people are tough and they are smart. Quite frankly, I fear for the future of our nation as long as they have the loudest voices. They want you to hate the other side. The more polarized to their disposition you are the more likely you are to keep watching—as the brain is just tickled by hearing what it holds sacred repeated by brilliant people backed up by an army of researchers and technical editors.

If you have a partisan sickness infected loved one—cut out the below Media Political Spectrum Chart (MPS-Chart) and paste it on the wall nearest to where they consume their partisan drivel. If they listen to political talk radio while on the road, laminate and place it in the center console for easy reference. Because the chart does not discriminate in the pathetically standard and transparent way of accusing Fox News of being conservative OR the New York Times of being liberal, it will inherently break their default thought pattern.

This chart serves a vital purposes: To call out and label the partisan industry as such REGARDLESS of political persuasion. I for one am tired of hearing people allege political bias towards only one side of the media. To allege conservative bias in the media writ-large by citing Fox News or liberal bias in the media writ-large by citing MSNBC or the New York Times is simply insulting to the intelligence. It is time we as a nation have an honest dialogue on the topic—i.e. not led by those within the industry itself. It is also time we de-link any of these organizations and individuals from what we refer to as the "mainstream media" (especially given the plurality of independent voters in this country).

Before moving on I want to tell you from whom the quote is at the beginning of this chapter (i.e. the "unidentified historical figure"). It is from none other than Adolf Hitler. I was searching for a quote on the benefits

---

** Definition created by author.

of painting political opponents as one, and was instantly struck by the applicability of this quote to contemporary America. Those with the partisan sickness honestly believe that all opponents to their policies are part of one dubious and monolithic group. This is precisely what partisan pundits want you to believe and are therefore in the persistent business of not only labeling everyone as 'socialist' or 'racist', but of trying to paint the opposition in conspiratorial like terms.

The next time you hear a partisan pundit generalizing about their political opposition, notice it. Say to yourself, "this person is generalizing." The next time you hear a friend generalizing about their perceived political opposition, intervene. "YOU ARE GENERALIZING. If you cannot articulate the true arguments of both sides, your opinion is not legitimate."

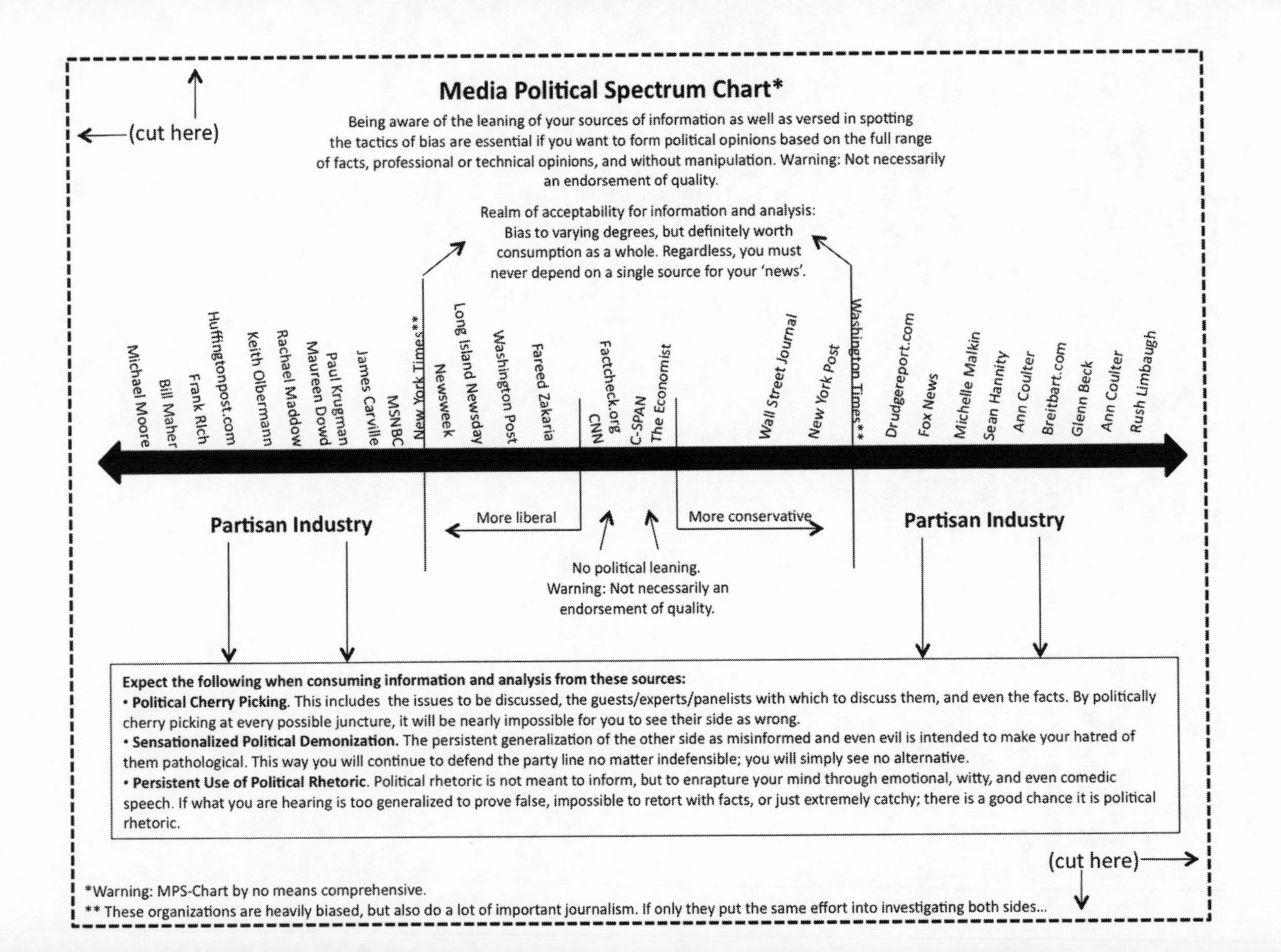
(cut here)
Media Political Spectrum Chart*
Being aware of the leaning of your sources of information as well as versed in spotting the tactics of bias are essential if you want to form political opinions based on the full range of facts, professional or technical opinions, and without manipulation. Warning: Not necessarily an endorsement of quality.
Realm of acceptability for information and analysis: Bias to varying degrees, but definitely worth consumption as a whole. Regardless, you must never depend on a single source for your 'news'.
Michael Moore
Bill Maher
Frank Rich
Huffingtonpost.com
Keith Olbermann
Rachael Maddow
Maureen Dowd
Paul Krugman
James Carville
MSNBC
New York Times**
Newsweek
Long Island Newsday
Washington Post
Fareed Zakaria
CNN
Factcheck.org
C-SPAN
The Economist
Wall Street Journal
New York Post
Washington Times**
Drudgereport.com
Fox News
Michelle Malkin
Sean Hannity
Ann Coulter
Breitbart.com
Glenn Beck
Ann Coulter
Rush Limbaugh
Partisan Industry
More liberal
More conservative
Partisan Industry
No political leaning.
Warning: Not necessarily an endorsement of quality.
Expect the following when consuming information and analysis from these sources:
• Political Cherry Picking. This includes the issues to be discussed, the guests/experts/panelists with which to discuss them, and even the facts. By politically cherry picking at every possible juncture, it will be nearly impossible for you to see their side as wrong.
• Sensationalized Political Demonization. The persistent generalization of the other side as misinformed and even evil is intended to make your hatred of them pathological. This way you will continue to defend the party line no matter indefensible; you will simply see no alternative.
• Persistent Use of Political Rhetoric. Political rhetoric is not meant to inform, but to enrapture your mind through emotional, witty, and even comedic speech. If what you are hearing is too generalized to prove false, impossible to retort with facts, or just extremely catchy; there is a good chance it is political rhetoric.
(cut here)
*Warning: MPS-Chart by no means comprehensive.
** These organizations are heavily biased, but also do a lot of important journalism. If only they put the same effort into investigating both sides...

Average Political Opinion—Characteristics and Facilitators

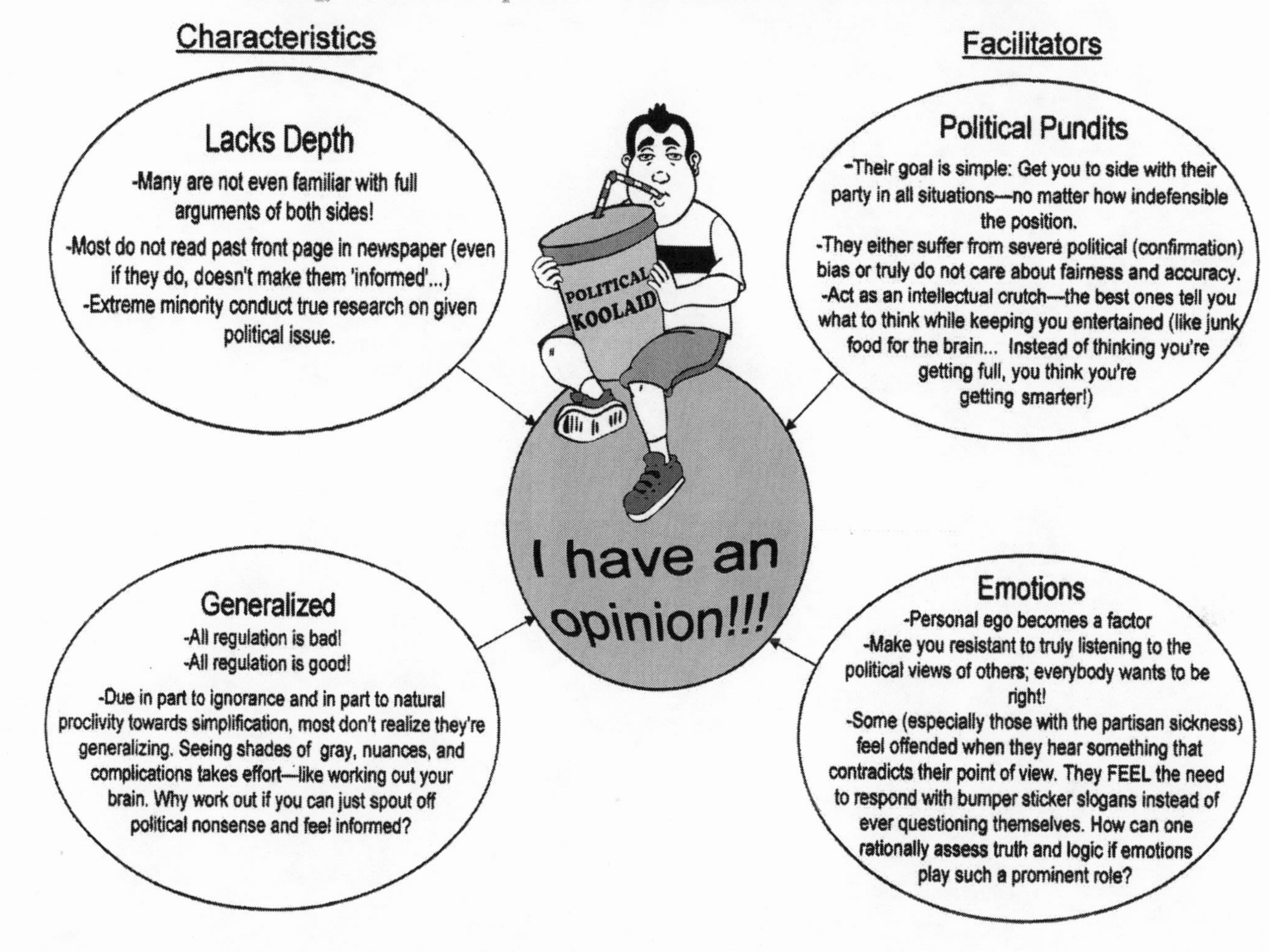

(To see enlarged versions of these graphics, please visit www.whatisbipolarnation/graphics.com)

CHAPTER 5: The Fallacy of Ideological Purity

The drive towards ideological purity within our society is creating a national false dichotomy and is therefore impairing our ability to solve problems on the national level. The notion that an ideologically pure government can comprehensively solve America's problems is a fallacy, in both political and practical terms.

Miss categorizations are a common occurrence when dealing with almost any problem, but especially vis-à-vis the highly complex or more generally that which we don't truly understand. By miss categorizing, we can become inhibited from truly solving a problem. While this is usually due to the exclusion of a category altogether, it can be due to any combination of miss categorization. If we don't carefully distinguish between problem sets as well as their solutions, or are too mentally pre-disposed towards one or two categories at the exclusion of others, we can be impeded from taking the most prudent course of action.

Let's say a boss asks a worker to write a report about how to better sell his company's product—widgets. Because the competition is selling a cheaper widget, the boss pulls the worker aside and says: "*I need you to examine the process by which we're selling our product A-Z. Find ways to be more efficient.*" What should be the first question from the worker? The first question should be about the scope of his research! Is he going to examine both the costs of physically producing the widgets AND the competitive costs of the salaries of the employees? What about the cost of his company's health care plan or shipping methods used to move the product? What categories of costs should be included or excluded from his report?

This is where proper categorization or lack thereof can result in loss. If the worker fails to take into account the problems emanating from just one area of the business, his analysis may be worthless. Likewise even if the worker asks the right questions, that doesn't mean his boss will have his categories—or at least intellectual flexibility vis-à-vis what those categories should be—in line. Should he arbitrarily limit the scope of the report and omit just one key area, the report may miss the forest for the trees. In sum, life is rife with opportunities to miss categorize, especially via omission, and by extension incur loss.

A specific type of miss categorization that often occurs when trying to solve a problem is called a 'false dichotomy.' It is the illusion that there only exist two choices when in reality there are more. In the given example, the worker would say "*well... our company must invest in either modern machinery OR hire more workers to maintenance those which we already possess.*" Now, a false dichotomy is only such if there are in fact other choices. In this instance, the worker's proposal would be a false dichotomy if the real problem actually stemmed from unfair competition, for example.

Perhaps the CEO of the main competitor is the brother of a Senator who is steering contracts to the federal government, thus enabling his widget company to use economics of scale in order to sell abnormally cheap widgets (not to mention unfairly fulfill the largest widget contract available). In this case, the worker omitted the category of "*corrupt activity in which our company could be engaging in order to give itself a competitive edge.*" The worker would likely be even more prone to this specific false dichotomy if he had an engineering vice business background, and would therefore seek solutions in the realm of that towards which he is pre-disposed (i.e. the physical process of producing widgets).

Now let's expand our analogy further. Let's say that to make the widget business more efficient, the worker believes that the manufacturing process, worker efficiency, and company benefits are in essence categories of things that can be adjusted. He then decides there are two basic solutions with which his boss can fix each one. Even though he is now exploring six options with which to improve the business, any of the two options per category could still be in themselves, false dichotomies. If so, the company is inherently going to suffer a degree of loss. This is why it is important for the worker to get feedback from a wide range of substantive experts and resist developing a confirmation bias towards his initial opinion. *He must entertain the possibility he has left something out and maintain the ability to rationally assess that proposed by others in order to maximize gain on behalf of his company.*

Now let's say that another worker was simultaneously given the same task. What do you think would be the chances that the two would identify 100% of the same solutions? Let's take it a step further: What do you think would be the chances that they only propose one solution for each category of problem vice three, four, or five?

Let us now consider the enormous societal problems to be solved by American politics. These problems impact over 300,000,000 people and yet in no area of life are false dichotomies more prevalent. They are so prevalent in this realm of problem solving because there are of course only two sides for each issue (whereas the worker settled on two solutions for each category of problem arbitrarily). In American politics our two sides are prone to miss categorize problems because they have preconceived notions for what is wrong with the world. And then of course, they have preconceived notions for how those problems ought to be solved. This is akin to asking a widget worker with an engineering degree to solve a problem emanating from his company's Human Resources department!

Both a symptom and a cause of our national false dichotomy are the partisan industry and political parties, which push the notion of a black and white world for monetary gain and political expedience. This sharpens the illusion that every issue is a choice between two narrowly defined political solutions; the only inhibitor being the other side's existence! And henceforth we often hear things such as: "You are either with us or against us!" "If you are against policy 'X' then you are racist!" "If you support policy 'Z' then you are un-American!" In the political context, such statements are almost always false dichotomies.

In today's hyper partisan environment many of those with the partisan sickness take positions simply because they are in fact diametrically opposite of those taken by the other side. In instances such as these we create false dichotomies for no other reason than pathologically ingrained political bias, whereas the factory worker would create a false dichotomy out of pure professional misjudgment.

In the realm of American politics we have broad or over-arching false dichotomies and then their sub categories and specific issues. Because ideological rigidity overshadows the entire range of categories into which all things political fit, we in essence have 'trickle-down false dichotomies.' We must intellectually be either a Democrat or a Republican, liberal or conservative. (Note that I said 'intellectually.' If you want to run for office and actually win you'd better choose a side.) Within the subcategories of foreign and domestic policy we must choose one of two generalized positions across a range of specific issues, such as for example nuclear proliferation or gun rights. Some issues, such as banking and global warming, cannot be placed in either sub-category because they are at once domestic and foreign. So keep your categories flexible! And beware the narrow presentation of two black and white politicized choices…

Now let's look at a real example. None will serve us better than the 2009-10 debate over health care reform. Due to the intense use of political rhetoric, political cherry picking, and sensationalized political demonization from all levels of the partisan universe (that comprising the partisan industry and the partisan sickness infected masses), millions of Americans bought into a false dichotomy. This false dichotomy was that in order to fix our mounting health care crisis we had to choose between tightening control over the insurance industry OR some sort of nebulously defined increased competition. (I label the Republican position as "nebulous" not as a criticism of the position itself, but as a criticism of the way that message was conveyed. It was never really clear what they were proposing).

This false dichotomy undoubtedly varied for different individuals amongst those with the partisan sickness. For some on the left it may have been akin to: "*We must control the insurance companies OR people will continue to suffer*." For those on the right it was possibly: "*We must stop the President's reform OR become a socialist nation*." Regardless, the net impact resulting from this grand false dichotomy was the same:

National False Dichotomies = National Loss; Continuous National Loss = Strategic Decline

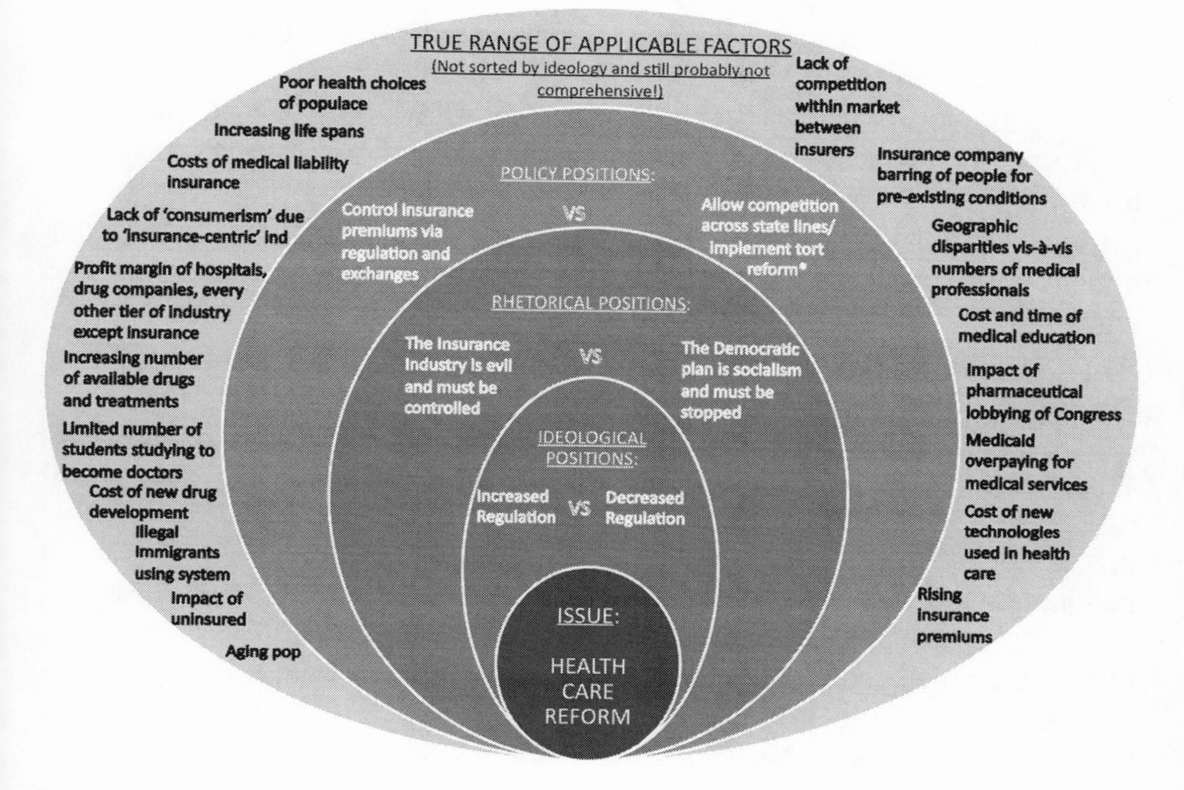

(To see an enlarged version of this graphic, please visit www.whatisbipolarnation/graphics.com)

If we were to interview a wide range of professionals involved at various levels of the health care industry and ask what they thought the 'real problem' was, we would likely ascertain too many factors to fit on the page.

***Tort Reform: An example of how pathologically engrained partisanship can cause people to take ideologically contradicting positions.**

- Most Republicans want to limit the liability of medical professionals in order to lower their insurance premiums and by extension make health care more affordable. But why should free market principles not apply to decisions made in the courthouse?
- Most Democrats defend the status quo in which medical malpractice lawyers make millions at the expense of the health care system writ large. Why is it unethical for insurance companies as well as a broad range of other stakeholders to make profits from health care while being perfectly legitimate if you're a lawyer?

We as a nation miss categorized the problem via multiple omissions and will therefore suffer loss. We miss categorized the problem because we examined it through ideological lenses. Because many of the real problems did not fit into the pre-conceived ideological worldviews of either party's base, we failed to discuss them altogether.

As had been stated, the followers on both sides are not just pre-disposed towards devising certain types of solutions for problems but towards seeing certain types of problems altogether. Conservatives gravitate towards terrorism and security issues, liberals towards social injustice and perceived inequality. This is why if one party is empowered we're not only more likely to try and solve certain problems, but we'll do so using pre-disposed ideological methods vice that which is supported by careful study and analysis.

This is why we went to war thinking the aftermath would be a cakewalk. The ideologues talked us into believing a grossly simplified paradigm in which the power of Democracy would erase a history of religious and ethnic division. More recently we allowed our hyper partisan dialogue to thrust a political false dichotomy upon one of our most pressing national issues.

Other Examples of Political False Dichotomies: Like any logical fallacy, they're in your head! However, these particular false dichotomies happen to be shared by millions and therefore influence or perpetuate national policy. In failing to properly categorize a problem or in these cases suffering from an outright logical fallacy (that there only exist two choices when in reality there are more), we inherently incur a degree of loss. It is my hope that these problems will illustrate not only the extreme simplicity with which we have our national debates, but how pathologically ingrained partisanship on both sides is hastening America's strategic decline. If we want to adjust and thrive in the 21st century, we must break our intellectual deadlock.

One of the categories on the following chart is 'foreign policy' writ large, as opposed to a specific issue within that category. Critics of the current administration's foreign policy are starting to argue that President Obama's brand of 'over-conciliatory diplomacy', i.e. talking, has borne no fruit with Iran, North Korea, or Myanmar. They're stating that the former administration's policy of threatening the use of force is preferable. And henceforth we as a nation have debated along partisan lines for over two years about how to best accomplish our international goals. Do we talk more while threatening sanctions or do we threaten more while threatening sanctions?

Issue/Category	Liberal	Conservative	National Loss	Non-Mutually Exclusive Policy Choice(s)
Health Care	Regulate insurance industry/public option	Increased competition/tort reform	Costs continue unabated, fail to comprehensively address problem	Regulate dropping of existing patients, mandate coverage, enable greater competition, greater use of health savings accounts, incentives for cost cutting innovation
Energy Policy	Support alternative energy/penalize fossil fuels	More drilling	Drive up energy prices while leaving ill-prepared for sudden spike, failure to adopt + lead as world power	Comprehensive plan: More drilling, incentives for research into alt energy + cleaner tech for existing sources
Foreign Policy	'Euro-Centric' Foreign Policy	'Threat Centric' Foreign Policy	Lock U.S. out of influence via trade and relations over human rights, other transgressions of international law; provide rising competitors strategic advantage by perpetuating view of U.S. as international 'bully'	Adjust to 21st Century realities: Reduce military overextension; trade with all nations, focus on building relations with big developing powers. Crux of new foreign policy = Continued economic pre-eminence while reducing possibility of future great power war
Iran/Nuclear Issue	Talk	Threaten	Lock ourselves out of real (trade based) influence, provide advantage to would-be competitors China and India; appear as international bully to 99% of world	Communicate concerns in private, plan for nuclear Iran
North Korea	Talk	Threaten	Expose our soldiers to brunt of conventional attack, tie down forces/limit strategic flexibility for other conflicts	Cede brunt of conflict to richer, more powerful South; limit conventional footprint. Can support South w/air + sea power in case of conflict

While many Americans harbor the illusion of mutual exclusivity between the positions of both sides on many issues, only a very small set of narrow issues are actually so. These include mostly social issues in which we must choose between one position as opposed to its polar opposite. For example we either support or do not support gay marriage. We either do or do not support abortion rights. They are not false dichotomies because truly *comprehensive* 'third way solutions' do not exist.

But here's the thing, despite all the partisan noise neither policy has borne any fruit! Critics on both sides are attacking one another's means to the same ends and yet we have still not made any progress in relations with any of these countries. This should lead us to a logical conclusion: Perhaps it is the 'ends' that must change!

Let me frame the 21st century in a nutshell: There are multiple regional powers whose economies will increasingly comprise a larger share of global gross domestic product (GDP). Two of these—China and India—have the *potential* to supplant us as the world power by century's end. The sum total is that our ability to levy effective sanctions will consistently erode (not to mention it is arguable whether they ever worked or were ethical in the first place). So it is not that we are getting weaker, but that many of them are getting stronger.

Coupled with this economic reality is an insanely large perception gap between how the rest of the world views us and how we view ourselves. Now please don't shoot the messenger, because I certainly don't see us this way, but much of the world see us as an over aggressive meddling bully. I, like most Americans, believe we're the good guys. But this isn't about what you nor I think, it is about changing perceptions and avoiding bad outcomes.

If we hold onto the same policies—no, the same mentality—as the 21st Century progresses, we are going to increasingly be seen as a global bully punching above its weight. What we need to do is extract ourselves from as many overseas security related problems as possible. The cornerstone of a policy that will truly fit the 21st century should be to build as close relations as possible with large developing nations India, Brazil, and China while at the same time preparing for economic competition with those same powers; the likes of which we haven't seen since before World War II. We must mitigate—not eliminate the possibility of great power war ever again. For all the talk about 'post cold-war weaponry' and thinking, we are moving back into a world with the potential for similar such situations.

We should trade with every nation, including those about whom we're not too crazy. Not only should we do this with the goal of maintaining economic and technological dominance in the 21st century, but as a means of having real influence. We have very little influence over those whose policies we don't like because we don't trade! Our ability to impact these nations will only weaken as their economic trade with growing regional powers increases.

I am not arguing we should be an isolationist power nor am I arguing we should refrain from expressing our opinion. The Indians, for example, maintain normal relations with all (except arch-enemy Pakistan) and choose to express their views through diplomatic channels as opposed to publicly berating those with whom they disagree.[55] I'm just saying that we should change the ways we do things to meet changing times. We needn't choose between a naïve European like mentality in which we unnecessarily cede our power while being preachy about everyone else's internal affairs or a 'threat centric' mentality in which we see a boogieman under every rock (and then kill it).

---

55 "Quiet Diplomacy' – new buzz word in India, Pakistan diplomatic landscape." Asian Tribune, October 11, 2004.

It is important to state that the rigorous pursuit of the aforementioned relations with growing powers is not mutually exclusive with threatening sanctions or force against smaller troublesome ones. However, it plays into the hands of the powers of the future not only on a direct level (such as Chinese or Indian trade with Iran), but also vis-à-vis their ultimate quest to replace us. We cannot afford to be seen by so much of the world as the bad guy.

I posit to you that extreme partisanship coupled with the two party system not only cause us to make decisions within a false dichotomy all the time, but that the problem is growing with the influence of the partisan industry and special interest groups. True believers now cannibalize moderates for perceived transgressions of ideological purity. God forbid someone has an innovate idea or viewpoint!

Once a party's base has one of two solutions to a problem pathologically ingrained as ideologically correct as opposed to the epitome of evil, it becomes extraordinarily difficult for politicians on either side to comprise—no less change their opinions based on new evidence, fact, or changing circumstance. This ideological tunnel vision often causes us to miss the full dimensions of an issue or potentially the issue altogether—creating ideological blind spots.

Many Americans harbor the illusion that we must choose between two mutually exclusive ideological policy choices across a broad range of issues. Even more so, they harbor the illusion that their ideological choice—be it liberal or conservative, Democratic or Republican—can save America. Yet the reality is that if unabated, ideologically pure decision-making would destroy the American dream.

Reality without the Fallacy of Ideological Purity

While we have so far looked at how pathologically ingrained partisan beliefs can cause us to miss categorize problems and their solutions, resulting in ideological blind spots, as well as how partisan information creates and re-enforces confirmation biases, we have thus far disregarded the core issue between American liberals and conservatives.

As always I will not take sides, but I do not mean to convey that one should not have a basic belief on what the role of government should be. Without a well thought-out vision on the proper role of government, our society will simply drift into the unsustainable. What I mean to leave you with, however, is a more nimble mind. One that doesn't emotionally react with partisan rhetoric to every issue or cause damaging fights with fellow Americans.

So on the specific subject matter (the role of government), I will just leave you with two stories in order to make a general point. For the first time I'll delve into the realm of fiction—sometimes (okay—all the time) satirically so.

The year is 2199, it has been four straight decades since a Republican has held office in either the Senate or Congress (and even he would have been accused of having been a 'moderate' by today's standards). The progressive dream of an equitable and fair society has been achieved, and thus 'inequality' in any *perceived* form has been eradicated from every nook and cranny. The environment has been saved from the consumer culture that was once melting glaciers, unnecessarily consuming meat, and attempting to drill on *pristine arctic tundra*. Corporate creed and malfeasance have been regulated—rightfully so—into extinction.

David, the average American boy of the future, is about to get up for school. Just like every morning, his 'guardian' (which is a levitating, metallic, and round representative of the state—think disco ball), wakes him up.

The conversation goes something like this:

Guardian: He-llo Dav-id. It-is-time-to-go-to-schoooool. I hope-you have stu-died the leesso-nnn plan on what was once called "junk-food."

David: Guardian, I still don't understand this "junk food." Why would anyone want to consume something referred to as "junk." I know I wouldn't want to eat garbage!

Guardian: You see Dav-id, it-is not-that the cit-i-zens did not want to re-sist the junk-food, buut ra-ther that they could-not res-ist. You must re-meem-ber that *during* the pre-re-en-light-en*ment*, pri-vate "***coorp-or-a-tions***" distrr-ib-ut-ed the food su-pply for ***pro-fit***. The *junk-food* only seeeerved the pur-pose of the ***pro-fit***, and had no **so-cial-val-ue**. It was "***mark-et-ed***" in such a manner that-the con-su-mer could not re-sist the taste or even-the-app-ear-ance of the juuuuu…

David: —but I still just don't understand why citizens would eat something called "junk" that turns them into fat…

Guardian: *Eh-eh-ehhhhhhhhh* Da-vid. You know that the term "***fat***" is a der-og-a-tory term for-which the state has gone through great lengths to re-place with: "OUTLINE CHALLENGED". Speak-ing of which Da-vid, you are nearing your car-bone foot-print for the quar-ter. You must-only con-summe one allo-t...ment of org-anic govern-ment ce-real bites for the re-main-ing 10 days.

David: But I hate—
Guardian: *Eh-eh-ehhhhhhhh* Da-vid. ***Hate*** is a strooong wooorrrr...d that was pro-li-fic dur-ing the pre-re-enlight-en-ment. I will re-trieve the-water for your ce-reaal bites.

(ADVERTISEMENT) "ORGANIC GOVERNMENT CEREAL BITES! They now come in the shapes of memos, filing cabinets, AND Al Gore! ORGANIC GOVERNMENT CEREAL BITES... the progressive (*and only*) choice!"

Story #2: The year is 2199 (again). It has been 100 years since the great American Re-Revolution in which the political right seized control of power and exiled the liberal elite to... France... *yes... France*. What was most surprising about the Re-Revolution, was the spark which set it off. Although the tax rates had long surpassed 50% on the average family of four making $50,000 dollars a year, it was actually a change in the McDonalds menu which re-ignited what was once referred to as The 2nd Civil War.

McDonalds, long a target of liberal health activists, was forced to change the composition of its French fries due to health and environmental concerns (simplified into one and the same decades ago in order to make change more palatable to the masses). This by extent changed the taste to something much closer to those sold at... Burger King (yuck!). Predictably, zero prominent political pundits predicted this series of events.

Although self-identified Republicans only composed 10% of the population at this point in time (the Democrats were themselves down to 19%), the Great American Re-Revolution only lasted 72 hours. The liberal hordes of "social scientists", health activists, and whiny yuppies were simply no match for the ex-military, mullet-wearing, burly *real-American* French Fry Freedom Fighters (The FFFF)—of whom there were much fewer. Geography also played a vital role in the conflict, as the Leftist Alliance was largely confined to four cities—New York City (in which the

NYPD sided with The FFFF anyway), San Francisco, Washington DC (in which The FFFF also contained a Trojan Horse—the Marine Barracks on 8th Street SE), and Austin Texas. Suffice to say, the Leftist Alliance' organic food supply was cut off immediately.

Given this series of events, the conservative dream of 'freedom' has long been achieved. Corporate America has broken the bondage imposed upon it by socialism (due to a series of mergers and hostile takeovers, there is now only one Corporation left). The environment is fine—as one usually cannot *visually* observe any discernable impact of pollution. Government is practically non-existent, and society has been brought closer to what it was during the first American Revolution… except with modern technology and 1,000,000,000 people. Freedom-Domes have been established in every town so that conflict can be settled without government intervention—so as long as both conflictees agree to forgo the 'public option' (i.e 'court').

David, the average American boy of the future, is about to get up for school. Just like every morning, he is awoken by his mother. The conversation goes something like this:

Mother: Are you excited to go to school today David?

David: Well, not really. Those bullies keep picking on me.

Mother: Now David, we've talked about this already. Those boys are obviously evil, as opposed to good. And what is it that we do to evil?

David: I know… *we punch it in the face…*

Mother: Now David, I don't want you coming home from school today unless one of those bullies are good and bloodied! I mean, how will you survive in the Corporation's world when you grow up?

David (*sigh*): Can I have some cereal?

Mother: Of course you can David, eat the whole box, its good for the economy!

David: Oh Ma! Not INORGANIC CORPORATE CEREAL BITES agaaaain! I hate—

Mother: Now now David, save your hatred for the enemy! Criticizing the Corporation is pre-Re-Revolution talk and I won't have it in this house!

(ADVERTISEMENT) "INORGANIC CORPORATE CEREAL BITES! They now come in the shapes of memos, filing cabinets, AND Rush Limbaugh! INORGANIC GOVERNMENT CEREAL BITES... the patriotic (*and only*) choice!"

Ideological Purity is a Political Fallacy because it is a Practical Fallacy...

Now think, aside from their bordering on science fiction, why can neither of these two futures ever become a reality? Because somewhere in between now and either of the outcomes, the American populace would vote the ruling party out of office or in these cases, rebel. Ideological purity in the American context, in which one party advocates more government and the other less, is not only a fallacy in the practical sense but in the political one as well.

You see, in the beginning of a political realignment, most Americans are willing to accept a preponderance of ideological policy because it is an antidote to a prior dose of inverse ideological policy making by the other side (or in response to large, detrimental event). In the short term that is what the citizens remember—the prior, inverse does of ideological policy or the detrimental event. They think to themselves: *This is necessary.* But alas, the collective has no long-term memory. And it is only a matter of time before that small group of anti-establishment centrists and independents becomes the majority, bringing us back to where we started.

This leads us to an irrevocable conclusion: The real interest of the American people lay with maintaining a semblance of balance between our nation's two primary political forces. The American people intuitively understand this. Henceforth the backlash that occurs whenever one party is overwhelmingly empowered.

And then there is the conclusion that can be drawn from the backlash itself: The ideological space between the hardcore partisans and the average American is significant—it is enormous. Henceforth the disdain of the ideologues towards the American people when they find themselves unable to implement their agenda in its purest form. In these instances, partisans are prone to blame misinformation or the public's lack of understanding instead of the policy itself. I assure you, it is the policy!

The bases of the both parties have deluded themselves into a fallacy. The fallacy is that if totally empowered, *their* party would solve all of America's problems and we would live happily ever after. What do they believe is the biggest impediment is to this end state? The other political party, its base, and during times of decline the American people themselves. The reality is that not only does too much ideology often cause us to miss issues altogether, but that either party's agenda implemented unimpeded would destroy our country. The true impediment to either group of ideologues holding of power indefinitely is the human condition. We yearn, no need a society that has a semblance of balance…

Both sets of ideologues believe there is some definitively perfect end state to which only their ideology can bring us. And yet it is impossible to articulate precisely where the line would be drawn in either society between where the government has a role to play and where it does not. You see, the human mind is wired to expect answers, to expect solutions. From the day we can speak we're taught to deal with simple problems in which there is always an answer, always an ending. 1+1=2, we can choose one of three methods to accomplish action 'x', and every story has either a good or bad ending.

Naturally, we believe there is a describable and sustainable end state that fits within our respective ideological worldviews. And yet there is no answer. The debate over how much government we should have is meant to go on forever. It is a story with no ending—akin to asking "where did we come from?" or "when did the universe begin?" Things that have no answers or conclusions throw the human mind into fits. And you know what? The fact that the current story—the debate over the right mix of government—is still going on is a good thing! If it ever stops it can only mean that a fascist or communist government has taken power—*and we'll all be eatin' the same cereal if that happens*.

CHAPTER 6: Will The Real Majority Please Stand Up?

Hyper partisan thinking and information are hastening America's strategic decline. Political polarization will at best result in strategic loss and at worst national disaster. There are things you can do on a personal as well as societal level to positively impact the future of our nation.

Throughout my time writing this book, I've been thinking: How did things get this bad? How did America become a country that hates itself? How did we enter this grossly simplified black and white world?

I have come to a diagnosis. Our bipolar state is the result of the nexus between difficult national times—a contested national election, 9/11, the Iraq War, Hurricane Katrina, sharp changes in commodity prices (especially oil), the housing bubble, the subsequent bailouts—with the unprecedented availability of our two core political persuasions in their purest forms via the partisan industry.

Whereas unprecedented common access to the same sources of information have caused a clustering around the ideological poles, the sheer increase in opportunity for the media to pick up outrageous and offensive commentary now consistently lowers our standards for what is acceptable political discourse.

The evolution of the 24-hour news cycle has incurred great changes in how the news is presented. While it may have started with the simple reporting of developments and facts, the networks very quickly evolved in order to garner higher ratings, not to mention fill a 24 hour cycle as opposed to one or two hours. This evolution took us from the simple reporting of developments and known (or thought to be known) facts to analysis, and finally to the Jerry Springer like version of political analysis we see today.

On a related note, I believe the 24-hour news cycle by its very nature perpetuates the belief that society as a whole is somehow worse off than it really is. It garners the perception that society and even humanity is actually on the decline, especially amongst the older generations. The reality is that we simply have much greater access to information, the lion's share of which is negative.

The Media vs. Perceptions of Society

Encompasses the full range of reportable events, developments, and stories in a given time frame.

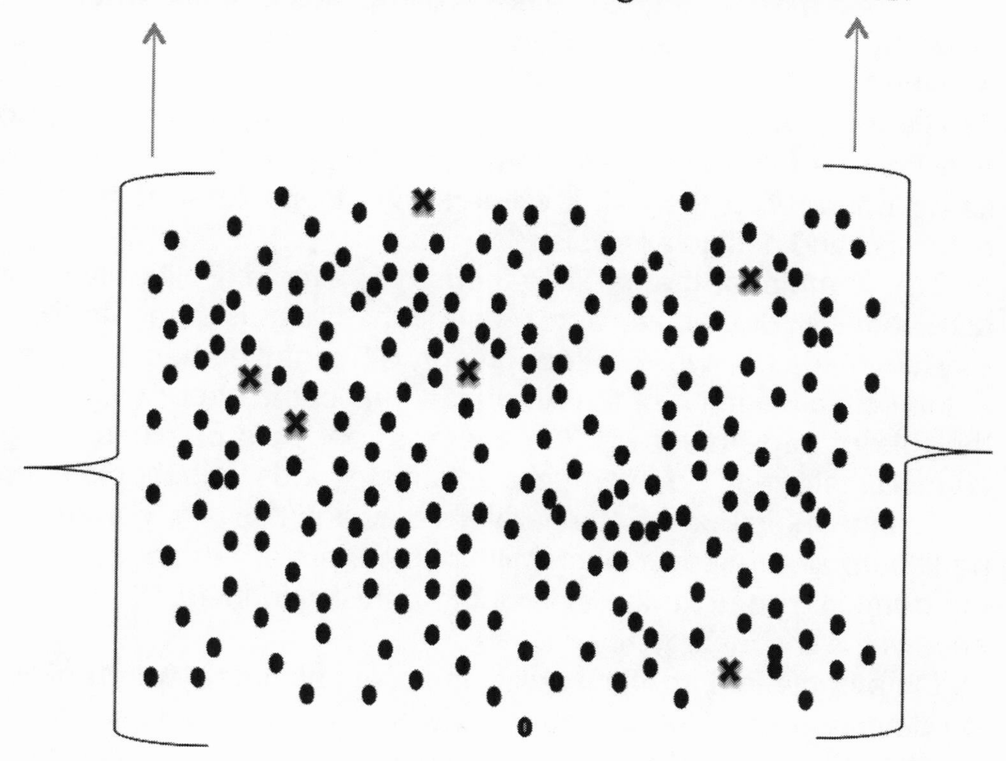

● = Positive or un-noteworthy development. Examples include success of U.S. manufacturing plant, increase in average SAT scores within a school district, kitten being saved from tree.

✖ = Controversial, outrageous, or shocking news. Examples include police chase, U.S. workers loosing jobs under worst possible circumstances, kid in remote part of Florida poisoning all cats in neighborhood.

✖✖✖✖✖ ●✖ = News reported during given time frame.

In seeking to present something people will watch, listen to and read, the media inadvertently makes the anecdotal appear as the norm. In other words, it doesn't always report when a factory opens or succeeds wildly in the face of foreign competition. It reports when one closes under the worst possible circumstances. Unfortunately it is up to the viewer to consider the possible reams of silent evidence that exist on any given issue.

This is not to say the news should change, because it won't. It is to highlight the impact it will have upon the individual if he or she allows it to. Consistent absorption of unrelenting political cherry picking not only makes one more prone to the partisan sickness, but probably also more beset by pessimism and anxiety in general. I assure you, the world isn't ending!

Given the new normal for the American media, I cannot see how we'll ever have a favorable view of another U.S. government. Regardless of its actions or lack thereof, it will face an inevitable stream of unfriendly reporting and hostile analysis.

The formula for the partisan industry is simple: Politically cherry pick, sensationally demonize, and present rhetorical arguments 24 hours a day, seven days a week. Although only a handful of their arguments stick in the collective mind of the American public, the sheer volume supports the rule of large numbers. On average, people's opinions are going to change faster and be ever more volatile towards whoever is in power.

I cannot help but see the parallels between this new domestic political battlefield and those in which military planners are engaged overseas. In the domestic context, the side of the partisan industry opposed to those in power is the insurgency.

On a battlefield in which agility is essential to deal with rapidly unfolding developments and the ability to wage a successful information campaign a critical important skill, the favor simply does not lay with the status quo power. This is because it is clumsy, slow, and must show tangible results or be forced to retreat via the whims of public opinion.

Amidst the messy unconventional conflicts in which the U.S. is most likely to be engaged, the probability of the media reporting an unfavorable story or fact—even if anecdotal—is far greater than the probability it will report something complimentary. This is especially true given the sheer size of the military apparatus, the natural inability to maintain complete control over such an apparatus (one of many "unknown unknowns"), and the difficult task of adjusting said apparatus accordingly to changes on the battlefield.

Consider this: A senior government leader is making sweeping changes to the way in which a war is fought or resourced. He or she decides to re-allocate $100 million for an alternative weapon system, decides upon a new engagement strategy vis-à-vis the natives of the occupied country, and then must speak before our allies with the goal of attaining greater assistance.

But then, a video appears on youtube of a U.S. soldier engaged in a grievous human rights violation. If comparing the tangible impacts of these things upon the direction of the war the latter should mean comparatively little. Yet the impact of it upon U.S. public opinion—that which is most essential for the complete implementation of the leader's strategy—is disproportionately large.

Now consider a similar example on the domestic political battlefield: A decision is made to bail out large corporations in our flailing financial sector for a variety of complex, uneasily digestible reasons for the American public. After implementation the media gets word that the CEOs of these corporations flew to meet with the President in luxurious private jets. The executives of the same corporations then decide to hold strategy sessions at posh resorts the day after firing 10,000 workers. It later turns out they were contractually locked into awarding large bonuses before receiving taxpayer money.

Even before the emergence of the partisan industry, any news organization would be tempted to focus overwhelmingly on the private jets, posh resorts, and bonuses. These stories require no substantive expertise to explain and garner ratings, particularly versus the more messy and subjective job of arguing that the bailouts had a positive impact on the economy. While all of these items are fair game for reporting and analysis, in today's environment many news organizations not only focus on the aforementioned negatives, but seek to deliberately ignore or minimize news that would bolster those to whom they're politically opposed.

From the point of view of the consumer who gets their news from an organization in the partisan industry (which is increasingly likely), this constant drumbeat of unfavorable facts and analysis constructs a pathologically engrained image of the other political side as not just incompetent, but potentially evil.

In light of the bailout example, please note that I am not taking a side on any of the aforementioned policies. I am merely arguing that given the natural proclivity of the individual to form confirmation biases combined with the existence of national news organizations solely dedicated to fueling them, is akin to having a permanent political insurgency against whoever is in power.

In the long term, expect partisanship to get worse. Non-partisan media is on the decline as the newspaper business fights for survival and impartial broadcasting for relevance. We also have an anti-moderate movement afoot in both parties by the respective bases to cleanse themselves of perceived ideological impurities.

But of course, none of the ideologues actually articulate their disdain for moderates in a manner that is straightforward or honest. To do so would border on political incorrectness. Instead, they accuse their own of being corporate cronies or closet liberals for perceived instances of ideological transgression. To those with the partisan sickness, 'moderate' has become a euphemism for 'traitor.' While partisan sickness infected individuals by no means represent the *real majority* of Americans, they have disproportionate influence via the primary processes and ideologically out of touch special interest groups.

Now that we have a diagnosis for what is causing the problem as well as a generalized prognosis for the future, we must ask ourselves another question: What type of damage can political polarization actually cause? What may America face as a result of what has become a deep ideological split in our intellectual and dare I say cultural consciousness, one in which region, religion, and even race play a role?

There is one thing for which I am certain: The ideological tunnel vision and subsequent national false dichotomies described in the previous chapter will continuously render us unable to truly gauge and address problems, not only hastening America's strategic decline amidst an increasingly competitive international environment, but often causing us to take international positions that are severely out of touch with said environment.

American power is set to face unprecedented competition from China, India, and even Brazil (not to mention the rise of a host of regional powers) over the coming years. The word 'unprecedented' can be used in this context because of the multifaceted nature of said competition, the likes of which the overwhelming majority of Americans have never experienced in their lifetimes. The Soviet Union was only competitive in one broad category of power: The military one. Due to their lack of an equivalent economically and technologically inhibiting ideology, our 21st century competition will be comprehensive in nature.

On a related note, you can expect partisan pundits to construct an overly simplistic 'cause and effect' narrative that ties America's perceived decline to the actions and policies of their domestic political opponents. The left will blame weak social safety nets and corporate hoarding of wealth. The right will blame over regulation and the 'liberalism' that has overtaken our society. Note that I nuanced my sentence about America's decline with the word 'perceived.' The impact of political polarization aside, it is not that America will be getting weaker in the 21st century, but that many of 'them' will be getting stronger.

Anyway, this hastening of America's strategic decline is the middle outcome—that which lay at the nexus of fair probability combined with fair amount of loss. There are three general ways in which it will unfold:

1) Because both sides are hardening around ideologically pure positions, they will pursue unbalanced policies that almost by definition incur a level of strategic loss when unencumbered by a strong opposition. If there is no forced balance of government, many legitimate solutions to our national problems will be jettisoned on the grounds that they don't fit within the ideologically pure paradigms of those who control the partisan industries, partisan think tanks, and primary processes. Concurrently, many problems will be ignored altogether for not arousing the ideological passions of the party in power.

2) But at the same time, politically balanced governments will be increasingly unable to compromise on key issues. The potent combination of common access to ideologically pure positions combined with the partisan industry led de-legitimization of one another's views will increasingly render compromise on key issues all but impossible.

What we see happening can almost be described as a dehumanization of both groups by one another's intellectual elites. This makes compromise psychologically difficult for the hardcore partisan, who has been convinced not only of the absolute righteousness of his cause, but that all opposition to it fits into one neat at best misinformed and at worst evil category.

3) Respective U.S. governments will increasingly seek to undo one another's polices on ideological, vice practical grounds. In the wake of 9/11 America responded by further empowering a very right leaning government, one that would give a befitting response to that terrible day. It did exactly that, in addition to implementing a range of ideologically driven

policies for which it had no mandate. In response we threw it out and overwhelmingly empowered a very left leaning government in a quest for change. We then got that change, in addition to a range of ideologically driven policies for which there was no mandate.

The political elites within these parties appear to mistake each empowerment as a mandate for their ideology, when in reality America was just throwing the other guy out of office. Independents and moderates, the first of whom now represent a plurality of American voters according to at least one survey taken in late 2009[56], almost intuitively counter react when they perceive a preponderance of ideology in their governance.

And thus it appears that not only are our governments increasingly left OR right wing, but that we may be going through political re-alignments faster than ever. This is due to the increasing severity of the ideology of those likely to be elected and the increasing speed with which the *real majority* moves to counteract them. Its speed intensified and arc widened, the traditional American pendulum has gone bipolar.

A new definition of politics amidst this era of rapid and acute ideological empowerment could be something akin to "*keeping a critical majority content enough to NOT vote you out of office while trying to implement your TRUE ideological agenda.*" Except it seems the ideologues in both parties would rather go on respective suicide missions than actually listen to what the American people are saying.

The problem for the purposes of this discussion is the practical impact of the respective empowering of such strongly ideological opposites. As we swing like a violent pendulum from Right to Left and back again, each respective government will bear enormous pressure from its base to undo the prior's policies on ideological, vice practical grounds or even those in the national interest.

In the realm of foreign policy this could make us particularly vulnerable, as we are already viewed as untrustworthy long-term partners by the elites in many countries for a variety of regional and historical reasons. If the bases of both parties continue to hate one another so strongly, what is to stop a newly elected majority or President from scrapping the prior's trade or even military agreement with a foreign power?

This is particularly plausible because the bases of both parties increasingly view America as having completely different roles in the world. This could create perceptions amongst our allies and enemies alike that we

56 Independents Take Center State in Obama Era: Trends in Political Values and Core Attitudes: 1987-2009. The Pew Research Center for the People & the Press, May 21, 2009.

are in fact a bipolar, and therefore undependable or weak actor. And again, as the 21st century progresses we will increasingly cease to be the only game in town for a variety of strategic needs.

In addition to these theoretical processes through which we may experience strategic loss, more immediate and vital national danger may exist where a few key issues intercede with deep ideological fault lines on both sides of the aisle. These issues if unsolved, will not only incur increasing damage with time, but can actually ignite social instability under the right (or wrong) circumstances.

The first such issue is undoubtedly illegal immigration, which the Arizona episode has so bleakly reminded us that we ignore at our peril. And yet what makes the issue so dangerous is that we are going to do precisely that. Entrenched partisanship on both sides has ensured that we will further delay serious action, and yet the longer we do so the more difficult it will be to solve. This is because the ranks of illegal immigrants will only grow, thus making mass amnesty even more unpalatable to voters while making the viability of meaningful deportation more unrealistic. The bases of both sides are clinging to increasingly unsustainable positions.

Very telling of our nation's deep political divisions on this issue were not only the economic boycotts by some cities and towns, but the inability of Arizona and the federal government to work together. Without taking a side, the division between certain state governments and the federal one on this issue are simply astounding. No, they are alarming. We must ask ourselves what this bodes for the future.

What will happen if a federal or state government ceases funding or cooperation with the other because of a disliked, but legal policy? What if an issue such as this were to cause a large enough group of citizens or even a state to withhold federal taxes? In this specific case, what if strong action on the issue by a future administration spawns mass disobedience by the other side? Rigid enforcement of immigration law or mass amnesty could do exactly that.

Given their access to increasingly ideologically pure information, we must acknowledge that large groups of Americans on either side could be convinced to take action into their own hands. This alarming episode should highlight more than any other that the possibility of social instability is real—even in America. At the risk of sounding like a broken record, the root cause is the consistent access to ideologically pure information, the infection of millions by the partisan sickness (an acute form of political confirmation bias), and their respective demands for ideologically pure but irreconcilable national policies.

The second issue that may harbor national danger is the debt. There increasingly exists a disconnect between those who think the debt is simply the result of the rich and corporations not paying their fair share of taxes versus those who believe we have a quasi socialist government leading our nation to ruin via a cycle of taxation and spending. Not an ideological coincidence, the first group sees nothing wrong with the perpetual growth of government while the later sees the ability to drown it in the proverbial bathtub as a desirable end state.

Essentially, when there is an argument about the immediate cause of the debt, the two intellectual contestants are usually engaging in a much broader debate over the proper role of government in society. The increasing disconnect over this issue, which lay at the core of nearly all American political discourse vis-à-vis domestic issues, is the result of two simultaneous but inverse movements within America's intellectual consciousness: One towards the more Democratic socialist model espoused by the Western Europeans, and the other towards the more libertarian version of America thought to have existed during the time of the founding fathers; both of which encompass the ideal amongst their followings.

Given the ideologically pure individuals who are likely to be empowered on both sides of the aisle in the future, the danger emanating from this issue will grow manifold if the right absolutely refuses to raise taxes while the left to meaningfully shrink the role of government.

If left unfixed, we will eventually face economic pressures that have the ability to cause social upheaval. It is uncertain whether those on the right will accept more taxes, as they'll conclude that we're merely prolonging the issue, feeding the beast, and deferring another debt crises to the future. It is equally uncertain whether those on the left will accept a meaningfully paired down government, as the long term consequences of an ever growing one seem to be perceived merely as the stuff of right wing conspiracy.

So really, we may be headed for political deadlock on our most immediately pressing issue—particularly after the next few election cycles. The reason we can be more optimistic on this issue than immigration is because there exist policy avenues to substantially reduce the debt that do not trip either side's ideological fault lines. This includes the raising of qualification ages for entitlement programs—particularly because the argument can be made that this is simply the result of increasing life spans.

That said, the problem stems from the fact that in tandem with any sweeping changes to how entitlements are distributed, some programs will have to be cut and some taxes will have to be raised. Should there fail to be compromise, the debt will balloon, our bonds will be downgraded, interest rates will dramatically rise, and a grave set of economic consequences will follow.

For example, the housing market may re-re-collapse (no that is not a typo). Because it is 50% true, the intellectual elites and partisan industries on both sides would blame one another. Those on the left will tell their followers that 'the rich' and corporations didn't want to pay their fair share of taxes. Those on the right will tell their followers that liberalism destroyed the country via an unaffordable and unsustainable European style government.

And aside from these two specific political issues that may harbor national danger, there may also exist unforeseeable causes of political upheaval. Specific sparks in history can almost never be predicted. And henceforth the great controversy that ensues following events previously believed implausible or more likely unseen altogether.

The reason why nobody can truly predict the future with any kind of precision is that specific events are impossible to foresee. What we can see however, are the trends that enable those specific sparks to significantly alter the course of history. Think of the trends as gasoline and the sparks as, well, sparks!

For example, one can predict that in 20 years two countries will have a relationship more defined by competition than cooperation. Such a prediction can be made based on a growing mutual exclusivity of their strategic interests. One can see that they are increasingly in competition for political advantage on their immediate peripheries, bidding against one another for natural resources, and increasingly purchasing weapons systems specifically intended to combat one another. What nobody can predict in such a situation is the specific spark that would cause these countries to actually engage in conflict.

Given our growing domestic political divide, there may be several sparks that are simply unpredictable. With the growing reliance on ideologically pure information via the partisan industry and subsequent entrenchment of hyper partisan thinking amongst the populace, the trends are certainly there. Future sparks could erupt over education policy or even a prospective national response to a foreign adversary. The growing political divide along regional lines in particular, could lead to any number of volatile permutations.

But it is not that some form of national political instability is a forgone conclusion, as it is actually improbable. But nevertheless given the trends, unimaginably bad outcomes are plausible. And regardless, hyper partisanship is hastening America's strategic decline via unbalanced policy and indecision. And thus, we must change the trends. The trends must be attacked and undermined. The partisan sickness can be defeated, and YOU can be part of the cure. But we must take the fight to where it actually exists: In the minds of our fellow Americans. The partisan sickness occupies the brains of friends, relatives, and co-workers; and no, this is not a zombie analogy. We are talking about working to change their mental images of society through sound argument and reason.

For these purposes, there are things we can do on a personal as well as a societal level. There are no silver bullets, but we must begin the long hard slog to bring political moderation back into vogue. We begin this process by bettering ourselves. This is because maintaining a nimble mind is like maintaining a nimble body: It requires constant practice. But even more importantly, without being truly equidistant at least emotionally, you will be unable to effectively challenge the views of your fellow Americans. You must truly be able to see the misdeeds of both groups in order to positively impact the national debate.

And then there is also that little thing called truth. You must persistently remind yourself that if you feel emotionally beholden to one side then you will loose your ability to rationally assess political issues. If you are unable to rationally assess political issues, then you are willingly depriving yourself of truth. Personally speaking, death is preferable to lack of truth.

So, consider this to be your partisan sickness immunization, for you yourself cannot deliver the immunization to others unless you are truly cured. This doesn't mean you can't hold views that are more amendable to one side or the other. Nobody is telling you not to have an opinion, but that you must make a clean emotional and intellectual break if you are to pursue the unblemished truth. Here is what you can do on a personal level:

1) Actively resist the temptation to politically generalize. This may sound simple, and even unsophisticated in so far as advice is concerned.

And yet, even the most brilliant amongst us do it. The gross political generalizations we all make only perpetuate the sorry excuse that is America's political discourse.

So if you find yourself about to make a generalization about a political party, policy, or political individual, stop and ask yourself if you truly understand that about which you are about to speak. Admit you may be generalizing and therefore do not have all of the necessary information to make a sound judgment.

Searching for nuance, distinction, and shades of gray require that you fight your natural inclinations—constantly—and rise to the level of something better. Admitting how much you don't know is a virtue, not a sign of stupidity. In front of others, it is a sign that you are intellectually mature. It can also be liberating.

2) Admit you don't agree with a few (or one to start) specific political positions of your own party—and then take those positions in the presence of the opposition. At the risk of sounding redundant, if you can't think of one then you clearly aren't thinking for yourself! If this is the case, again think of the sheer improbability that one of only two ideologies has the answer for every problem. Also remember that there is no comprehensive ideological glue between all of the positions on either side.

Admit your position while in the company of someone with the partisan sickness of the opposing ideology—an overbearing conservative uncle, a liberal yuppie aunt who lives in the city, your father who is obsessed with Glenn Beck, etc. Prove to yourself that you can have a civil debate, calmly agreeing on some positions while disagreeing on others. No matter what happens, do not respond with political rhetoric. We cannot ask our nation to rise to something better if we ourselves cannot refrain from being bipolar when with friends, relatives, and co-workers of the other ideological persuasion.

3) Eliminate or balance the partisan industry as a source of information. Remember what it is these people do: They profit from the deliberate distortion of political issues in a manner that grabs your attention and garners ratings. If you agree with their politics you can expect their opinions to sound good. They do this primarily through political cherry picking, which is the deliberate selection of data that supports the preferred ideology while ignoring or minimizing that which undermines it.

If you want to honestly pursue truth, you must at least diversify your news input. If you watch Fox News, also watch MSNBC and vice versa. If you read the New York Times, also read the Wall street Journal and vice versa. A good test of whether or not your informational input is balanced, or even beneficial in the first place, is whether or not you can actually articulate the true viewpoints of both sides. If you cannot, your opinion on the issue is null and void. The false characterization of both sides' positions by the other is pure poison for the mind.

To defeat the poison you must find the cure. One example of a truly non-partisan source of information is C-SPAN radio. Instead of paying lip service to being fair and balanced, it seems they have made a conscious decision to listen to the complaints of both sides vis-à-vis bias. Some would say C-SPAN is not entertaining (unless you count the callers), but you can get much greater fidelity on an issue by listening to congressional hearings or extended interviews with substantive experts (as opposed to the seconds you get on television). Not a day goes by where I don't listen to C-SPAN and re-conclude how little I understand about a given topic.

You can also listen to the aforementioned callers and ask yourself an honest question: Is that how I sound? Am I that rhetorical? Do my generalizations contain as little substance? This will further the impetus to understand both sides before blurting out a so-called opinion.

Factcheck.org is another great resource. Its staff corroborates or debunks popular political conjecture on whatever the hot issue happens to be during the given timeframe. If the media is rife with a controversial political issue, chances are factcheck.org can somewhat clarify the situation. There are also countless other highly informative sources of political information, but you have to want to find them.

While on the topic of balancing one's sources of news, I also challenge you to do an exercise: Watch your favorite partisan pundit and identify examples of their utilizing the three broad tactics of political persuasion outlined in chapter 4. Catching a celebrated partisan pundit of your own predilection engaged in political cherry picking, sensationalized political demonization, or persistently relying on political rhetoric is the ultimate intellectual liberation. Your true sense of impartiality will be permanently aroused, owing to the realization that there truly exists less than pure motivations on both sides of the aisle.

Now we move on to the broader fight. While we must constantly exercise our own brains in order to pursue truth, the fight must ultimately be taken to those of our fellow citizens. We go out into society not with guns blazing or torches burning, but with reasonable arguments, a soft tone, and an honest desire to challenge the status quo in a constructive manner. Here is what you can do on a societal level:

1) Attack the mental paradigms of those with the partisan sickness. Although you are likely to encounter stiff resistance and fierce counterattacks, the point of making these arguments is not to defeat the partisan sickness instantaneously, but to sow the seeds of doubt in the patient. Arousing one's objectivity is a process—as was their drift towards an ideological extreme in the first place. I find the following to be particularly effective:

When an individual takes the same ideological point of view across a diverse set of issues; challenge them to explain the ideological glue between those views, and then question whether it is possible they simply have a confirmation bias. The average person has never been challenged on the broader issue of how they think, and is instead mired in unending narrowly focused discourse. This is the ultimate missing of the forest for the trees. Ask them: *Is it possible you're simply incorporating and emphasizing the evidence that supports your beliefs while ignoring or minimizing that which does not? If not, how is possible that you agree with one political party on every issue despite their having nothing to do with one another?*

Remind them of the grave ideological contradictions of both the contemporary American liberal and conservative ideologies. Explain that because there is no ideological glue across all of their positions, it proves that a comprehensive believer simply has a confirmation bias as opposed to being informed. One could argue this is even more so the case for those Left and Right Wing individuals who are so much so that they don't even identify as Republicans or Democrats. In fact, it is the only possible explanation.

Attack their entrenched mental paradigm through the 'probability argument.' Ask whether they've considered the sheer probability that only one of two ideologies can have the answers for all of society's problems. Challenge them to think of ANY policies of the other side with which they agree. If not, explain that the partisan sickness is *a condition in which the patient has a prepackaged negative judgment of any and all actions of the members of the opposing political party; often resulting in unpleasant dinner party conversations, emotional arguments, and a higher than normal usage rate of the terms 'fascist' or 'communist' (currently being substituted with 'racist' or 'socialist').*

Persistently challenge the legitimacy of the organizations in the partisan industry; do so with resolute impartiality. It is time that those who condemn FOX News while ignoring the misdeeds of MSNBC and vice versa are called what they are: Hypocrites. Don't be afraid to say it. Multiple sources of news on both sides engage in the same exact behavior, and yet their followers use ideological righteousness to shield their misdeeds.

Ask your fellow citizens if it is a coincidence that they take a nearly comprehensive liberal or conservative point of view AND get their information from these sources. If not, is it possible they're just re-enforcing their own views by getting information from a like-minded source? Explain that the partisan industry is defined as *those who seek to profit by selling a particular political point of view in a biased manner; usually accomplished through the emphasis of news and information that bolsters the preferred political point of view*. In other words, they simply show you what supports their ideology.

Convey that it is okay to be a moderate and that we don't have to choose between two increasingly extreme ideologies. This alone will defy the ideological paradigms which now define the mindsets of so many of our fellow Americans.

The perception of moderates amongst the hardcore partisans is that we lack the conviction or attention span necessary to support a policy through implementation. What it has really come to mean however, is that one has the sound judgment necessary to weigh evidence and reach conclusions based upon data, as opposed to having a preconceived notion for how a problem ought to be solved. To be a moderate amidst this climate of partisan lunacy is to be reasonable, fair, and levelheaded; not a political traitor or intellectual lightweight.

It is time that moderates take a stand and moderation be defended. Lest not, America's intellect be ceded to the howling, bias lunatics on Fox and MSNBC. Should you pursue the path that is political moderation, you can state that you believe in a balance between the liberal and conservative ideologies—that they both have their advantages and both have their drawbacks. You can state they are both necessary.

Don't allow the most extremes amongst us to be the most oft heard! Say it! I AM AMERICAN, I AM MODERATE, AND I AM PROUD OF IT!

2) Work to empower political moderation. While reasoning with our fellow citizens is aimed at combating the partisan sickness in the individual

and by extent healing the nation, there are also things we can do to directly impact it. I have neither the space nor the will to list them all, but you can start by:

Supporting the least ideological candidates on both sides of the aisle, and letting people know exactly what you're doing. It is moderate problem solvers that will navigate America through tough times, solve vexing national issues, and properly calibrate policy in order to best position it for 21st century strategic competition. And yet these people will become a political dinosaur if the populace doesn't demand differently. Even if you do not abandon your party and register independent, stand for moderation wherever it is you already stand. Should your party nominate an ideologue, have the courage to speak out in front of your peers and defect.

You can identify the least ideological candidate by looking at their voting records and life experience. Look to past language and political rhetoric for clues to how they really feel. If a Republican candidate campaigns heavily on fighting terrorism, family values, and the 'lie' that is global warming—he cannot be trusted. If a Democratic campaigns heavily on ending tax breaks for the wealthy, stopping the evil health insurance industry, and halting domestic drilling for oil—he cannot be trusted.

Please remember that I am NOT taking positions on any of these issues. There is no set combination of issues that can lead one to conclude a candidate is or is not an ideologue when compared to their opponent. What one need look for is a steadfast adherence to the party line. Such intellectual rigidity is symptomatic of the kind of decision-making that gets us into trouble through imbalanced or misplaced policies. On a more elementary note, it is also indicative of one's inability to think critically. Even worse, true ideologues are so self-righteous; they do not want to think critically. For them, considering other options is merely a political façade for public consumption.

Making civility a priority within your peer group. You can agree with an elected official or even partisan pundit on 100% of the issues (and I will allege that you have a confirmation bias), but that support should not extend to circumstances of severe disrespect or unnecessary combativeness towards the other side. The other side should be respected and their positions fully understood. Just look at some of the things that have been said during the last two years, and ask yourself: Is this the America I want to leave to my kids?

> *You lie!*—Republican Congressman Joe Wilson during the President's speech on Health Care Reform, September 9, 2009.[57]

> ... *they* [conservatives] *want Obama to get shot*—Ed Shultz, [liberal] radio talk show host, August 13, 2009.[58]

> [President Obama] *has a deep seated hatred for white people*—Glenn Beck, [conservative] host of "The Glenn Beck Show", Fox News, August 13, 2009.[59]

> *Well, the answer to that is, they're assholes*—former White House Green Jobs Advisor Van Jones on Republicans in February 2009 (while he still occupied the post; previously he admitted to being a communist).[60]

If a friend or relative is demeaning the other side, call them on it. Explain that they're not only failing to sway the minds of others, but are actually pushing them away. If you see an elected official or partisan pundit engaged in such behavior, write a letter, turn off the TV, cancel your subscription to that paper, and speak against it. Civility isn't going to return because we close our eyes and wish it so; it is going to return if elected officials and media personalities pay a price for incivility! If we want America to change we must become impartially intolerant of vitriol.

Supporting 'ideologically transcendent', or 'third way' solutions to our most vexing national problems. Elected officials and future administrations in particular have an opportunity to mitigate the impact of extreme partisanship. But they must be willing to buck party ideologues who will accuse them of selling out for mere compromise with the ideas of the other side. On that note and primaries aside, compromise is more than the right thing to do; it is good politics.

Regardless of whether moderation resurges within the conscience of the populace, our problems will remain. In order to move the nation forward, politicians can put forth truly innovative, ideologically transcendent solutions to America's most intractable problems. In other words, such

57 http://www.latimes.com/news/nationworld/nation/healthcare/la-na-wilson10-2009sep10,0,2959545.story; last accessed September 17, 2009.

58 http://www.realclearpolitics.com/video/2009/08/13/liberal_talker_ed_schultz_conservatives_want_obama_to_get_shot.html; last accessed August 14, 2009.

59 http://www.reuters.com/article/newsOne/idUSTRE57C07920090813; last accessed August 14, 2009.

60 http://edition.cnn.com/2009/POLITICS/09/06/obama.adviser.resigns/

solutions must be at once very liberal and very conservative. They must either not trip the ideological fault lines of either side or simultaneously neutralize their ideological fervor.

For example, perhaps we can tackle the immigration problem with mass amnesty as well as a massive and sustained deployment on the border. Or, perhaps we can issue biometric cards up until a certain date, but commit to actually deporting those who ignore the mandate. The key is to find a way to solve the problem practically and politically; as opposed to shoving heavily one sided solutions down one another's throats.

Should a future politician be reading this, there is a key ingredient necessary to actually formulate such policy: A professional, substantively knowledgeable, and non-ideological staff. It doesn't mean they can't have their leanings, as you're obviously not going to staff your office with your ideological opposites. But at the end of the day, they must be honest brokers of information and options, as opposed to closet ideologues merely viewing the contents of a problem with an eye out for what supports their beliefs.

Wrapping it up...

I leave you with this: Liberals and conservatives must learn to appreciate one another's contributions to society or we face a grim future. The notion that we can thrive without one or the other is a façade, a scam pushed by hardcore ideologues unwilling to see any good in one another. Not only does the far left and right both contribute vital ideas, but they actually fulfill vital functions. Liberals push for equal treatment under the law, keep corporate malfeasance such as environmental degradation at bay, and bring us art (sorry for stereotyping). Conservatives keep our corporations competitive, our taxes low, and enable America to defend itself by joining the military (sorry for stereotyping).

In the American context they are like two mildly competitive symbiotic organisms on an animal's back; while they are in competition, they are both necessary to the animal's survival and therefore that of one another. If you want that animal to survive, build immunity to the partisan sickness, cure it where you see it, combat the partisan industry by highlighting how it operates, push for compromise via ideologically transcendent solutions and a moderate 21st century America!

Much has been said about the seemingly imminent decline of the U.S. Yet it will only decline commensurate with its inability to think of new ideas, be they pertaining to our role in the world, how we approach foreign powers with which we disagree, or our ability to solve systemically critical domestic issues. Any country is only as stagnant as its thinking, the future as dark as one's inability to innovate.

We also must not allow the notion of others getting stronger to depress our spirit or national morale. Instead, we must embrace the 21st century for the new challenges and prospects that it brings forth. For too long we've lived on the laurels of those Americans who came before us. And thus we've forgotten that to be great, one must earn it. The civil rights leaders of the 1960's, the generation that stormed the beaches at Normandy, and the founding fathers weren't brought up being told they were great simply because they were American; they made America great through blood, sweat, tears, and ideas!

It is time that we rise to our challenge, for future generations will look back at this time and have one of two narratives: Either we pulled it together and solved the most intractable problems of our day through fresh thinking and COMPROMISE, or became mired in domestic political dispute and watched the world pass us by. What will you do? How will you make America a better place?

I for one will fight to keep America on top, but that fight starts at home. For if we cannot be a nation of moderate problem solvers, then we will be a nation of immoderate problems. Decline starts at home. I for one, will represent the real majority…

Epilogue

An unsustainable ideology is inherently unrighteous. What is most important is that you are at least attuned to the problem…

In reading this book, one could easily get the impression that I am against the idea of having an ideology writ large. Quite to the contrary, if one does not have some semblance of vision for what functions a government should and should not perform; it will simply drift into all while accomplishing none. What I have spoken out against is the pathological adherence to ideology or the taking of positions while disregarding of evidence, facts, and the gamut of potential solutions.

So ponder this: The far left wants a more domestically interventionist government and the far right wants one that is 'limited.' Yet regardless of how liberal or conservative an individual claims to be, one can always find theoretical situations with which to make that individual question their beliefs. Ask a conservative who advocates extremely limited government if his neighbor should be able to keep 100 dogs in the yard adjacent to his. Similarly, ask a liberal if the government should be able to exert the same control over security that he wants it to vis-à-vis social welfare.

But why is this? Why is it that any seemingly reasonable political ideology can be made to look foolish or contradicted? The reason is because there is no perfect political ideology, none without flaw or shortcoming, none that cannot be found inadequate in some situation. The world is simply too complex, as the number of scenarios are literally infinite that will call for some permutation of decision making, be it political or legal, not previously considered. And of course many political ideologies are just completely flawed.

One argument I will make is that any political ideology that is unsustainable systemically—that is economically or socially—is inherently unjust. Communism always fails because innovation grinds to a halt and the system grows gross inequities within its ability to produce goods and services. Fascism on the other hand usually revolves around a single individual or cadre of military planners; neither of which is ideal for good governance given the lack of accountability and probability that a lunatic will eventually rise to power.

While I am not comparing the two sets, the sustainability rule can also be used to view our own liberal and conservative ideologies—and that is more or less all I'll say on the matter for now. The important thing is not so much that you choose or don't choose a basic ideology within our system, but that you keep sustainability in mind. So ask yourself, what will policy 'x' lead to? For what else does it set precedent? Is this going to overload or under-load the system and set it up for a systemic discontinuity?

On the issue of balance-of-government, I offer the following rarely repeated excerpt from former President Eisenhower's farewell address. While he was speaking primarily to the military-industrial complex, it has special relevance to the resurgent debate of our times; that about the proper role of government in the economic and social realms:

> Crises there will continue to be. In meeting them, whether foreign or domestic, great or small, there is a recurring temptation to feel that some spectacular and costly action could become the miraculous solution to all current difficulties. A huge increase in newer elements of our defense; development of unrealistic programs to cure every ill in agriculture; a dramatic expansion in basic and applied research-these and many other possibilities, each possibly promising in itself, may be suggested as the only way to the road we which to travel. But each proposal must be weighed in the light of a broader consideration: the need to maintain balance in and among national programs--balance between the private and the public economy, balance between cost and hoped for advantage--balance between the clearly necessary and the comfortably desirable; balance between our essential requirements as a nation and the duties imposed by the nation upon the individual; balance between action of the moment and the national welfare of the

> future. Good judgment seeks balance and progress; lack of it eventually finds imbalance and frustration.[61]

We must now ask ourselves one last logical question: If building an ideology and by extension a government that is sustainable, reasonable, and righteous morally and practically so difficult, then why is it that so many have bought into extreme ideologies throughout history? Why is it that so many are allured by ideologies that are not only unable to perpetuate progress, but often extreme and dare I say 'evil'? Now of course in the e-word context, we're not talking about America's own contemporary domestic extremes. They both impede solutions on many problems and are arguably immoral in many ways, but are in no way 'evil'.

But addressing the broader question, people are allured to extreme points of views, be they extreme ideologies or religions, because life is otherwise a never-ending process of discovery. We spend our whole lives with questions such as: Where did we come from? Is there a god? Is there life on other planets? What is the best system of governance? Questions such as these will persist to the end unless in your individual process of discovery, you happen to come across and become enraptured by an extreme point of view.

You see, broad explanation based points of views, regardless of the their manifestations, bring that so very frightening process of discovery to an abrupt halt. Suddenly there is no more curiosity, no more uncertainty, and above all, no more fear. For you have found an answer to all. Talk to an individual who believes deeply in an extreme political ideology or religion—a communist, a Christian fundamentalist, a radical Islamist, etc, and they all have one thing in common: They have the answers for everything.

Returning to our not evil but certainly troublesome domestic context, extreme leftist or right wing ideology provides a similarly succinct and comprehensive narrative for every single problem faced by our society. That is their allure: Extremism gives people a distorted sense of intellectual comfort. And hence, once someone is in such a mindset they'll distort reality to fit their beliefs rather than continuing that never-ending and at times scary process of discovery.

An individual or a people should have a basic vision for their system of governance, or lest it drift into all functions and fulfill none (more on that in the next book). This is a call for intellectual flexibility and a willingness

61 President Dwight Eisenhower's January 17, 1961 farewell address.

to solve problems within the context of facts, outcomes, precedent, and sustainability; but also within our own established political system and perhaps more importantly, the political standards and norms that have so carefully developed over the centuries. It is a call to not let fear control our actions. But intellectually speaking, we should be comfortable with fear. For if there is no fear, then we know everything. If we know everything, we have become extreme…

Made in the USA
Lexington, KY
20 October 2010